Inferno

Part Four of the Sistema Series

A DYSTOPIAN HORROR

ULTAN BANAN

Cover design by Ultan Banan © 2025
Editing by Seminal Edits

ultanbanan.com

ISBN: 978-1-914147-31-9

Inferno

I

There are silences that go deeper than silence.

The heavy steel door closed behind the boy, and on the other side, nothing. Not a whisper, not a breeze. Only stillness and darkness. Saleh stood for a second, a second which became a minute, and the longer he stood the more he seemed to lose himself. The silence and the darkness ate him; he felt himself pulled apart by it, yet he dared not disturb it. It ate him until he could stand it no more and he took a tentative step forward, a step which seemed to prompt the illumination of a single light above his head. The fluorescent bulb came on with a hollow clack, followed by the incandescent buzz of tube lighting.

The light and the sound overwhelmed him with relief, if a relief tinged with deep and indeterminate tremors of terror.

Another step forward, another light flickered on.

The boy walked forward, lights coming on one after the other above his head until the room was illuminated and the steady but unsettling buzz of white fluorescent tubes hummed around him.

He stood in a small room, twice as long as narrow, with a single table in the middle, four chairs, and a row of steel lockers along the wall to his left. Where he was exactly, he wasn't sure, but with the help of Verne and Eric he'd explored

System A for months now, and he was aware things were not always as they seemed. Things could change suddenly, without warning; the important thing was not to panic. He'd learned that now. Learned the hard way.

He moved to the lockers by the wall and began opening them one by one. The first was empty, the second too. In the third, a pair of overalls on a hanger. Below, a hard hat.

A couple more empty ones, then some pornographic magazines. Then he found a torch. He flicked the switch to test it, found that it worked. He slipped it into the pocket of his army jacket, the one like Caleb's which he'd bought after his friend was killed. He'd always liked the way it flew out around his friend as they chased each other over the rooftops of the city. He thought it looked cool. So he bought one, partly because he wanted one, partly because he thought it was a good way to honor his friend. Now, for this mission, it was his uniform. It gave him protection.

He opened another locker. Found an icepick inside. He picked it up and shivered, feeling its cold lethality in his limbs. As if his body understood intrinsically the damage it could manifest, how it could puncture, cleave, tear holes in essential organs. He put it back and closed the locker.

—Saleh?

The voice in his head made him jump. In the unfamiliarity of his surroundings, he'd forgotten he was not entirely alone.

'Verne? Is that you?'

—Jesus, kid. Thought I'd lost ya. Transmission is patchy. You hear me?

'Yeah. I hear you.'

—Where are you?

'I'm in a room. Like a waiting room. Nothing in it really. Found a torch.'

—How many doors?

Saleh looked around. The door he'd come in was shut. He knew it wouldn't open again. Straight ahead, at the opposite end of the room, was the only other.

'Just one.'

—Okay. Chances are you're at an entrance node. When you pass through the door you'll probably find yourself in some kind of security zone. I know we ran through this in training a million times, but there's no guarantee what you find once you leave that room. We've run all the security protocols we could dream up, but we've no idea how close we were to the mark. So be alert.

'Yeah, okay.'

—And most important – listen to that gut of yours. It never lets you down.

Saleh took a breath. 'I will.'

—If I cut out and you lose me for a bit, hang tight. I'll get back up soon as I can. But it may be that once you're inside, you're on your own.

'Okay.'

—When you're ready, go see what they've cooked up for us on the other side of that door.

Saleh didn't say anything. He checked his pockets one last time, feeling the heavy reassurance of the torch. Taking a last look at the door behind him, perhaps with small hope that Celeste might come through – a partner, someone to stand by his side – he nodded with silent acceptance that no, she was not coming, and this was a thing he had to do alone.

Saleh turned and walked toward the door, stopping in front of it and putting his hand on the cold steel surface, as if that might give some indication what lay on the other side. He felt nothing. Heard nothing.

He put his hand on the handle and pushed it open.

Hot air hit him like a furnace blast. And on that air a whisper was carried, reaching him and making his legs tremble:

'*Intrusion…*'

Saleh took a sharp breath.

—What was that? You hear something kid?

Saleh swallowed. 'I'm not sure. I thought I heard something. Probably nothing.'

Maybe his imagination.

Saleh stepped through the door and closed it behind him. 'Verne? You still there?'

A broken message came through. —… me, kid? You—

'Verne?'

The voice in his head fell silent. He guessed it would happen, but he didn't like being alone in this place. Maybe the connection would be restored.

'Can you see this place, Verne?'

Saleh turned his head slowly, looking at the unsettling vista in front of him.

He was standing in a room that stretched endlessly in every direction, filled with large cubes that seemed to glide over each other on three planes, forming a nigh-impenetrable maze like some vast living game of Tetris. From somewhere, deep-red recessed lighting illuminated the room. The cubes hovered effortlessly this way and that, only inches between them, now and again an aperture opening up within the vast wall to hint at hidden turns and nooks within.

Saleh had come face to face with some of the horrors Vathos could dream up. Eric's team had familiarized him with elements of the immersive program they knew only as 'Hell'; he hoped he wasn't in it right now, but the deep red of the lighting and the heat of the place made him think otherwise.

Yes, he had seen horrors. He didn't want to see more.

'Verne?' he asked once more. No answer.

He went cautiously down two steps onto the solid metal floor in front of the vast moving vista, where he stopped, waiting to see if he'd trigger some kind of alarm. When nothing happened, he advanced.

He moved forward until he was within arm's reach of the moving blocks. Now that he was close, he noticed that they hummed from within, emanating some kind of life force. He felt heat come off them too. He raised his sleeve to his forehead and wiped the sweat away. Looking over his shoulder, he noticed the door he'd come through could not be seen. All behind him had fallen into darkness.

He turned back to the wall of cubes that slid noiselessly over one another. They seemed like a hologram, yet he knew if he reached out and touched one he would find it solid. He did – put out a hand to test his hypothesis and felt the heat of the cube, felt some kind of vibration from within. He pulled his hand away. He knew not what this strange technology was. But then maybe it was just some kind of hologram – he was in a computer program after all.

He took a step back to glance up and down the line of shifting cubes. At that moment the cube right in front of him and the one moving in the opposite direction behind it parted to reveal an opening into the vast shifting maze within. The thought to leap inside flashed into his mind, but he hesitated, then it was too late. He waited; he knew the opportunity would come again. It did, a few seconds later, but now his thoughts were of being crushed inside the vast shifting array of enormous cubes. He hesitated again, and didn't take his chance. But now he noticed that the cubes inside seemed to be moving at a slower pace. He figured he'd be okay. He figured he could make it.

He moved closer to the shifting wall, putting out his hand to touch one of the cubes as it passed. He felt reassured by its solidity and vitality. When the gap came around again, he was ready for it this time. He saw it open up and without a thought leapt inside, the vast wall closing up behind him.

Now he found himself on top of a gliding cube, as if on some conveyor belt to nowhere. He was moving to his right; the line in front of him was moving left; the line behind that was moving down. Every second or third block a cube was missing, so he timed it, navigating the way ahead of him by small leaps and bounds. Two or three rows he moved forward like this, until he found himself on a stationary block, an island of sorts, where he could pause and take in his surroundings.

He felt like the red lighting had dimmed since he'd entered the cube array, and all around him things were getting darker.

He took a few leaps forward to test his perception; yes, the more he neared the 'center', the more the peripheries fell into darkness, as if the very act of moving was leading him toward an unavoidable locus.

This did not deter him. He moved on, darting in between cubes, until he leapt on one which immediately changed direction from a horizontal to a vertical plane.

He cried out in alarm. Down could not be good. He spun around, looking for way to get back up. He noticed through a gap in the alternately horizontal moving walls in front of him that several rows ahead was up-moving row.

It was a big dash to make. With no margin for error. He tried to glance down between the tiny gap to see what lay below, but saw only darkness.

A chance came, two apertures aligning to give him the opportunity to dash through, but hesitation killed his initiative. He cursed himself, and braced for anther gap to appear. He was getting deeper, and alarm began to overtake him.

Blood pumping now, adrenaline threatened to cause him make a grievous mistake.

Two openings suddenly aligned in the walls; he waited until sufficient of a gap opened to allow him through, then dashed, leaping through both apertures to land on the rising wall. To his dismay it shifted from vertical to horizontal, moving left. He put his hands in his hair and pulled.

Then the blocks to his left dissolved, and he seemed to be moving toward a platform of sorts. He saw a dim blue glow, and not too soon, for he was almost enveloped in total blackness. The blue glow reached out to meet him. The platform appeared to be moving toward him, like when an escalator nears its destination. At the last second he leapt off, finding his feet on solid ground.

He stood still for a moment, looking up ahead where there were two silver doors. In front of them, he wasn't sure... was it...?

In front of each door was an animal: one a monkey, unmistakably a monkey, for its animal howls upset the quiet hum of the cavernous emptiness he now found himself in. Except the monkey was blue.

The other... some kind of big lizard thing. It was huge. Saleh had never seen anything like it. The lizard was red.

They stood in front of their respective doors like two freakish sentinels.

Without warning, the monkey turned and looked at Saleh, raising a long finger to point in his direction. It squealed, causing the boy to step back. The monkey hopped up and down and spun around, taking a few frantic leaps forward in Saleh's direction. The boy darted back. The monkey squealed again, before hurrying back to his door. The large reptile stayed still and silent.

When he saw it wouldn't attack him, Saleh moved forward in slow cautious steps, stopping a safe distance from the two animals. Both the animals seemed to regard him for a moment, and the blue monkey gave one final squeal before settling down on his hunkers with unnatural tranquility. It turned its head to the red lizard.

The red lizard opened wide its mouth. Inside, Saleh saw a golden orb float there. A vibration seemed to emanate from it. Words followed, words that took shape like a lotus blooming in still water.

'Falsities rise from this garden like caryatids in an ancient entablature. Hidden intentions are the surest path to cruel barbarity. The hollow of these vaunted halls eats the incautious like the mad eat razor blades. How does your garden grow?'

Saleh stood unmoving, perplexed in his simple naivety.

'I don't know what you mean.'

Again came the disembodied voice he'd heard when he'd first entered the room, the one carried to him like a whisper on hot air. This time it said,

'Innocent...'

Saleh looked around for the source of the voice but saw

none. He turned back to the red lizard. The golden globe in its mouth had begun to spin.

'Do you seek entry to the House of Truth?'

Saleh looked to the silver doors behind the animals.

'I want to pass.'

'Through which door would you pass?'

Saleh spoke from someplace inside that didn't think and didn't analyze. 'Only the correct one.'

'And which is the correct one?'

'The correct one is the one I shall choose.'

The monkey's two hands were turned upward as if in bizarre meditation, or weighing two choices for which great consequences would follow.

'And if you don't choose correctly?'

'That would be incorrect, and therefore impossible.'

The lizard's head turned toward the monkey, and for a moment it seemed they were engaged in some unspoken congress. It turned back to Saleh.

'What color am I?'

'Golden.'

And what color is my companion?'

'Golden.'

At this, the monkey seemed to bow. Saleh raised a hand to his neck, unsure how to respond. The lizard was silent. The boy grew uncomfortable. Beads of sweat dotted his forehead. He became antsy. But remembering his training, he concentrated on his breathing and tried to stay calm.

'One final question,' the voice from the lizard intoned. He paused. 'What is at the end of all our travels?'

The boy swallowed nervously. 'Only certainty.'

The mouth of the lizard closed, and the blue monkey stood up on its two legs.

The disembodied voice came once again in the hot air. *'Choose your door,'* it whispered softly.

Without hesitation, Saleh raised a hand to point at the door behind the blue monkey.

'*Intrusion is only the first sin,*' the voice came again, this time as if from right behind him. Saleh spun around, but there was no one at his back. When he turned again, the animals were gone, and the door he'd chosen lay open into nothingness.

He supposed there was no way to go but forward.

2

The darkness went on for an eternity and more, an eternity that shuddered with the brutal awareness of time and its passing, and the relentlessness of that passing and the violence of it. The mind crumbled under that violence until mind was no more, only void and absence, and from that void came the knowledge that man, all he is and was, and all he builds and fights and dies for was naught, of nothing and for nothing. And with that, peace. All that came after, the reliving of it, life's battles and victories, failures and contempts, hopes and desires and loves – all that was Hell.

Vangelis Zervas lifted his head from the black earth in which he lay, and didn't know, didn't realize, the depths to which he had descended. He felt the void, though. The abyss in which he languished. Felt the weight of it like the weight of a thousand years on his shoulders. On his soul. A terrible, crushing weight that made it difficult to rise from the mud.

He got up on his knees. He didn't know where he was. Didn't remember how he came to be there. Didn't know who he was, until he ran muddied hands over his face, finding familiar contours and scars, an intimacy with his body that restored his sense of self. The void – the void he'd traversed to get there – came back to him, threatening to crush him. He thrust himself to his feet, as if the very act of using them might keep the great emptiness at bay. On his feet, he teetered.

Though he couldn't see, he could tell he was ankle-deep in thick mud. He strained every muscle, every fiber, to raise one foot and propel it forward. Then the other.

'Free me,' he whispered. Then louder: 'Free me!'

The sound of his voice was eaten by the very atmosphere. Swallowed. He screamed then, a scream of desperation. And of the suspicion that he was dead.

The scream was eaten and disappeared on the thick foul air. Vangelis became frantic, pulling at his limbs to free himself, only ending up on his face in the mud once more. He raised his face and screamed again. Terrified now. Terrified he was no longer alive, and terrified he might still be. That this was a place from which he might not return.

'I am alive!'

His shout met no ears. He struggled back to his feet and pushed on, each step taking years off him, until, tired and broken and feeling like he'd lived a hundred lifetimes, he put his hands on cold, hard rock.

He lay down. Rolled over on his back. Rubbed his muck-smeared eyes.

'Fucking help me,' he whispered.

He felt a hot stinking breath on his face. When he opened his eyes he saw the sneering maw of Maynes on top of him, a knife poised to slice into his eye.

He lashed out, his hands hitting nothing but air. He blinked, spun his head, but he was alone. Still, he thought he heard his boss's sneer.

It came back to him now: who he was and what he did. The company he worked for. The mission. The confrontation in the woods – Maynes with the gun pointed at him. Celeste. Celeste firing at Maynes. Then a large beast attacking her and dragging her down… here. To this place. To this hellhole, whatever it was.

He had to find her. If he had to do one thing, only one, it was find Celeste and make sure she got out.

He slid back til he was resting against a rock. The thought of getting up caused him to close his eyes. If only he could lie here – what harm would it do? He'd been through… what had he been through? He wasn't sure, he just knew his mind bore the scars of ages, his body the weariness of the ancients. If he could only just sleep.

A bolt of pain shot through his head and caused his body to contort, his hand going to his temple. He shook his head and swore. There was no rest here. None. He knew it. He knew he had to keep going until he was either out or dead. He turned, rising onto one knee then up to his feet. He put a hand against the stone wall. Immediately he felt it soften, his hand slipping into the fleshy, clammy surface. He pulled it away, and turned to follow what he thought was the direction of the wall. Still fumbling his way forward in darkness, he reached out tentatively at each step to glance the wall (now hard rock again), careful he did not commit to the touch.

The cavern – it felt like a tomb – seemed to close in around him. His claustrophobia increased, and he soon found his head touching the ceiling. He moved forward on his hunkers, then on his knees, and before he knew it, he was enclosed on four sides by close rock. When he tried to go back, he found he was stuck, and the only way he could proceed was by moving forward. Soon he was sliding on his belly through a cold dark tunnel, his elbows close into his sides, the rock scraping his shoulders. He stopped, his breath labored.

'I didn't want this,' he whispered. 'I didn't ask for this. Where the fuck am I? Let me out of this fucking hole…'

He'd only moved several more feet ahead when he became stuck. He was sweating now, the sweat dripping over his mud-caked face. His heart beat faster. His knees, his elbows, his shoulders, were all pinned by hard cold rock. He felt it press on him. Closing in. And the more he panicked, the tighter it seemed to get. As if his breathing was somehow in sync with the environment around him.

He fought to stay in control, to calm his mind. But it was

too far gone. The rock pressed tighter. He felt his body begin to cave in on itself. He felt his bones press together, his organs become compressed. Pressure on his brain. Pain exploded from every atom inside him, all at once, at a million points in his body. Right as he felt he was about to pop like a meat-filled balloon, he screamed.

The rock around him suddenly changed consistency. It was no longer rock, but flesh. It contracted and expanded like a large pulsing intestine, Vangelis lodged inside it like troublesome foreign matter. The flesh enveloped him each time the intestine squeezed tighter, constricting Vangelis to the point of suction. He slid down the slimy tube with each contraction, the slick walls facilitating his descent. Head to toe in mud and now greasy with the sputum of the immense throbbing organ, he slid like fecal matter down the chute, the passage becoming tighter, until, with a final murderous constriction he was shat out with terrifying force as if from some horrific anus.

He landed in a thick, suffocating pool of shit.

Breaking the surface with a desperate howl, he struggled through the noxious excrement until he once again found solid ground, pulling himself up and falling on his face. He spluttered, then pulled himself to his feet and ripped off his clothes: jacket, T-shirt, trousers all. Naked, he stumbled forward toward the shaft of light emanating from the darkness up ahead. The source of the light was unclear, but where it struck the rock it seemed a door materialized. Vangelis drew close, stopping to behold the strange aperture. He looked back over his shoulder, seeing only darkness.

Then he turned and walked through.

There was a blinding flash. Next thing he knew he was standing behind a waterfall. Not believing his eyes, he reached out to touch the cascade of water falling before him. It was cold to the touch. He stepped in; the water came down over him with a thundering weight, threatening to force him to his knees. He resisted, running his hands through his hair until he was free of filth. When he was fully cleansed, he waded out of the water and up a series of steps. Above him, a cavern that rose for miles into blackness. At the top of the steps was another door. Exhausted, he opened it.

Inside, in a darkened room draped with purple velvet and lit with a single lamp, sat a woman in a purple velvet armchair. He closed the door and gawked at her as if at a mirage. The woman was not old, not young, was dressed in a blue robe and had a kindly face. She peered up at Vangelis with bemusement, then gestured to a chaise longue in front of her. Vangelis stepped forward, looking at the chaise longue then at the woman with trepidation.

She put her hands in her lap. 'Your journey has been long,' she said. Her voice was like velvet honey; Vangelis felt his limbs unwind.

He took a halting step toward the chaise longue. If he could just lie down…

'You have caused much suffering. But you too have suffered,' the woman intoned. Her voice penetrated to the very soul.

Vangelis choked up, felt tears rise to his eyes. The woman patted the chaise longue. Vangelis put one knee on the cushioned bed. Then he crumpled onto the soft velvet, curling up in the fetal position. He wept profusely.

The woman reached out and stroked his face, and ran her hand through his damp hair.

'Tell me,' she said.

Vangelis shook his head. 'I can't. I can't…'

'Shh now.' The woman dabbed at his tears with a finger, then ran her finger over his lips. He tasted the salt of his tears. Felt it moisten his parched lips. He felt his cock rise. Raising a leg, he attempted to hide his erection. The woman stroked his face and issued soft maternal susurrations, her hand moving to his ear to play with his lobe. Desire, rising in him like a tide, overcame the despair and the shame. The woman got up from her chair and moved to the chaise longue, sitting down next to him. Her hand moved to travel over the contours of his back. He felt the heat of her heavy thighs through the coolness of her silk robe pressing against his. His erection strained now against his belly as the woman's hand glided down his back, onto his buttock and down his hard thigh. He shifted onto his back, exposing his hard cock to the gentle hands of his succubus. Her hands now on his chest, his belly, then on the inside of his thigh. She stood and lifted her robe, pulling it up around her waist to expose heavy haunches that guarded her soft, odorous sex. She sat down again, allowing Vangelis to run his hand up the expanse of her inside thigh until it found her sex, wet and open, velvetsoft. He slipped a finger inside, then two, her hand on his hard cock now and pulling softly, Vangelis closed his eyes and moaned like a man dying, and when he was ready she climbed up on top of him, straddling him with her heavy thighs, guiding his cock to her soft velvet sex and letting him slip in. 'Home,' she whispered, putting her mouth to his ear and spilling gentle divulgences into his ear as she slid down on him til he filled her whole, her sex causing his cock to engorge to unknown proportions, like the limb of a tree. She took his bottom lip between her teeth and bit until he bled.

'My sweet baby boy,' she whispered, and Vangelis opened his eyes to see his mother riding him gently, her eyes gazing at him with a mother's pure love.

It took him a second to realize. Then his eyes opened wide and put his hands to her face, but it was too late. He felt the lips of her vagina turn to teeth sharp as razors and close around his cock until, with a short tug, it was ripped clean from his belly.

He gaped down to see blood spurt from the bloody hole. His mother put her bloodied lips to his ear.

'Sweet, sweet boy…'

Her tongue slipped from her mouth, as it did it morphed into a tapeworm that worked its way inside his ear until it was burrowing inside his brain. He screamed as the worm expanded and his brain exploded as if thermite had been ignited inside his head.

He saw red. Then white. Then he saw no more.

3

'There is a way.'

The disembodied voice spoke as if carried through the very floors and walls.

But as Saleh gazed at the vast maze of servers blinking like a myriad unsettled galaxies, synapses in a vast brain that formulated god-knows-what dangers, he did not see a way. The server stacks formed a walled garden, nothing less than a true maze, imperious and impenetrable.

'How? How can I pass?' Saleh shouted into the air.

The voice responded with its unhelpful platitude. *'There is a way.'*

Saleh looked to his left, shrugged and walked along the line. The room he was in was vast, cold and clinical, lit only by the flashing lights of the servers. A reticulate hum emanated from the machines, as if some ancient intelligence resided within. And Saleh did not want to infuriate it. He moved cautiously.

His training in System A had been grueling. To start with Verne had merely thrown him in and let him run loose to discover for himself the peculiarities of the 'Principle', as Verne sometimes called it; it wasn't exactly a computer program, but it was accessed through complex digitized biometrics over which software could then be laid for the engagement of various endeavors. Eric and his team used it mostly for training purposes, but it could also be tuned to facilitate espionage, and it was also how the operation financed themselves. They didn't go wild with it; they weren't engaged in any major heists, they just stripped away a little liquidity here and there where it wouldn't be noticed – such as with investment firms where the numbers were in constant flux. Like this, they underwrote their operations against Vathos. They saw nothing wrong with it, neither did Saleh or Celeste – they thought it was entirely right, since they were only stealing from firms who hired Vathos to engage in bad things. Evil things. And Saleh knew, even at his young age, what evil was.

The training had started innocently enough. Saleh had enjoyed exploring the vast expanses of System A, but it wasn't long before he discovered that System A wasn't a place you could play around in without, at some point, coming up against the deepest, darkest parts of yourself. Since System A was what Verne and Eric called the 'metaconsciousness', your own consciousness was an inextricable part of it. At least that's how Eric described it. He finally understood when things from his past, even his childhood, began to crop up while he was exploring the vast latitudes of System A. The first thing was the sobbing. When he'd lived in the tenement before his parents were killed, next door to him was a boy a few years younger who lived with an addict 'carer'. It wasn't his dad, maybe an uncle or something, but the uncle beat him, a lot, and forced him to steal and do things no child should do. Through the thin walls of the tenement Saleh heard the boy sob. Not every night. Some nights he would rage and destroy stuff. But when the rage had burned itself out and it still didn't get rid of the grief he carried deep down, the boy cried. Alone in his room, he cried and cried, and all Saleh could do was listen through the walls. Some nights it was too much and Saleh put on his sister's earmuffs when he went to bed so he wouldn't have to hear. He felt guilty about that. He felt guilty he'd never reached out to help. Never once knocked on his door. And even when he saw the boy outside, he would turn his face away and not make eye contact.

What might have happened if, just once, he'd met the boy's frightened and violent stare? Had the courage to see his pain and not turn away from it? Might he still be alive?

Hearing that sobbing for the first time in System A made him realize the metaconsciousness was not a place for fun.

There was also the dead child he'd found in a bin one night when he was out exploring the city. He was only eleven years old. The baby kept appearing while Verne was running Saleh through training, and it didn't stop until one time it occurred to him to approach the baby and close its eyelids with his fingers. After that, the baby did not come back.

There were other things too. Lots with his mom and dad, but he didn't like to think about that. He pushed that stuff down, and that's why it came back all the harder.

Some things he would never get used to.

'There is a way.'

He looked up when he heard the voice, and thought he saw something disappear between the server stacks. A flash of what looked like a small human.

Saleh hurried toward whatever he'd seen, keeping to the middle of the aisle, afraid something might leap out at him.

He reached the gap between the servers, pausing to peer inside. There was a way in, and if someone, or something, had disappeared through it, he could to. He stepped into the gap.

There was no doubt about it. He was in a maze.

With only one direction to go, he followed it, taking a left turn then a right.

He saw the flash again in the distance. This time he made out a figure: the figure of a small girl. He froze. She looked once over her shoulder at him then scurried away.

'Wait!'

He took off after her, reaching the end of the aisle and turning right. She ducked around another corner. He sped up, but around each corner she only seemed to evade him.

And where was she leading him? Out of this maze, or deep into its impenetrable core?

Realizing he was now lost inside and probably couldn't find his way out if he wanted to, he stopped. He considered his dilemma. Try and go back and get more lost, or go forward after the child? And still end up lost.

Right then he heard the frail voice of a little girl singing. He walked in the direction of the sound, following it around first one corner then another. Finally he took a right turn and saw the girl at the end of the aisle. Standing between server stacks which towered either side of her, she looked minuscule. She wore a shabby nightdress and held a worn-looking rag doll by the arm, the other arm of which hung down to the cold floor. The child was shoeless. Something about her caused a knot to form deep in his belly. He felt like he knew her.

Saleh was afraid to take a step forward. He didn't want to alarm the girl. Without breaking her song, she turned from him and looked up at the server stack next to her. Saleh, emboldened by not having her eyes on him, took a step in her direction.

He didn't know the song she was singing, but he could make out the words: '...*innocent when you dream...innocent when you dream.*'

Somehow it touched him.

As he neared the girl, she turned to him. He stopped. There was no fear in her eyes. She merely pointed at the server stack. Saleh took it as an invitation for him to come and look, so he drew close, close enough to see what she was pointing to.

He stopped next to her and followed her finger.

'This? Is this what you're pointing to?' He put his finger on a MicroSD slot on the server stack.

The girl, her eyes a timeless twinkling brown and her face etched with a kind of timeworn knowing, nodded.

'What should I do?'

The girl lifted her teddy and turned it to show Saleh the back.

'You want me to open it?'

The girl nodded.

Saleh took the doll from her. It was as tattered-looking as the girl herself, and now that Saleh held it in his hand he could see that the doll's dress, the print on it worn almost to invisibility, was of the same white and blue striped pattern as that worn by the girl.

The back of the doll had two buttons on it; Saleh opened them to expose the stuffing within. He pushed his fingers inside. Buried there was a MicroSD card. Saleh pulled it out.

He pointed at the slot on the server. 'I have to put this in here?'

The girl took the doll from him and hummed softly. '…*innocent when you dream…*'

Saleh looked at the SD card then at the girl. He was torn. He'd lost his best friend after he'd stuck a dangerous card into a mystery device he had no knowledge or experience of. If Saleh knew one thing, he knew this could end badly.

'What is it? What will happen?'

The girl clutched her doll and turned from him, her eyes scanning the servers around her. For what, he had no idea.

He looked hard at the tiny card in his hand. What choice did he have anyway? He was in deep now and still had no idea how to negotiate this place. Maybe he was in the place Verne called the 'firewall'. The firewall was a security system built around a computer to keep bad stuff out. And if this was the firewall, who was the little girl? Maybe she was one of bad things trying to get in, and was only using him to get what she needed. Anyway, maybe he was 'bad' too, in some way. He wasn't supposed to be here, he knew that.

All he had to go on was his gut. He'd listened to it thus far, and he was still alive. He was listening to it now, and it wasn't telling him something bad was going to happen.

He took the SD card and raised it to the slot, and with a final look over his shoulder at the little girl, he put it into the machine.

In the flicker of a second, blackout.

Lights went out all around them. The servers went dark. The girl was no longer singing. Saleh put a hand on the server stack to ground him somehow to his surroundings.

'What just happened?' he whispered.

The girl did not answer. But lights came on, a deep red, which cast a haunting glimmer over the cold, sterile server room in which they stood. Saleh looked down to find the small girl looking up into his face with a seriousness that terrified him.

Then the piercing scream. Followed by another. Screams that caused a cold fire to rise up his spine.

'What the hell was that?'

The girl did not break eye contact. She raised a straight arm, finger pointed, to indicate behind him.

'They are coming now.'

4

feel me rape your fucking mind, fucker, i will eat you from the inside, i will devour you like fire, rip through you until all is scorched, you will never wake from this annihilation, or maybe i wake you and do it again, motherfucker i'll rape you over again, and then? let's bring your mother, fuck her like your daddy never did, cause he was a son of a bitch but not a god like me, and he couldn't bear to look at her after he conceived you he still went out and fucked her sister. let's get together, your mother father and i, we'll make you watch, see me fuck your daddy's face? see me rape his mind until he shits himself. watch me rape your mother until your daddy gurns. what about your sister? i know your incestuous dreams. i once lay down with a spent whore and pored poison into her ear for a day, and when i was done she murdered her four children and burned them in the firepit. i ate their charred corpses and spat out hymns. want to hear what i sung? i sang of gluttony and the beauty of it, and watching a child starve while i filled my fucking face, and the silence of joy and the music of rage, the contendedness of consumption and the neverending pit of human capital. i sang of the innocence of children and the emptiness of innocence raped, and the rape of innocence was the highest note of my serenade, and when i hit the high notes birds fell from the trees and old men put razors to their throats, and the spent whore impaled herself on a redhot iron poker until her shriveled womb was burned like kokorech on the spit. I EAT YOUR FUCKING WOMB, CUNT! with a little salt it's just right, but not as good as the spent placenta of a raped virgin. i will eat you all day, you little cunts of goodness and faith. i bestow on you the grace of annihilation, for in it there is salvation. am i not your salvation? am i not the one of whom is spoken? i am not the shadow, even if before me falls the murderous umbra which draws out your insides like a soul enema. *thhleuup!* i suck it out of you, i can suck it out through your asshole, feel your lifeforce leave you demonquick, feel you drain until you are nothing but skin. i climb inside your skinsuit, masturbate myself dressed as you, fuck your loved ones dressed as you, murder, fuck, rape and plunder dressed as you in your pathetic skinsuit then i discard you like an old halloween costume. but what am i saying? i was raping your mother, yes, yes, now i lie down next to you real close, you feel my nipples hard and hot on your painted back, my tongue at your ear, my cock like a crucifix poking at your thigh, and i tell you your life story from birth, how they lied to you and fed and starved you and gave you what you needed but not what you desired, and how they molded and pushed you, and how they beat you when you didn't do what they wanted, even though they were motivated only by pride and greed, and you are the bad child! bad child, bad bad child, does not do daddy and mommy's bidding, sick infantile, fetid creature, oh but they love you, they do, they do it for your own good, and you are good because you do it for your sister, you love her and you do it for her, all for her—*incestfuckincest*—really you do, your shining light she is, your moon on a dark night—*sisterfuck*—if only she was another woman and you another man—*eatsistercunt*—and there was no blood between you—*fuckfaceruinsister*—ah, but you were good the two, knew good from bad, and she met a nice man and you, well you, well we know don't we, but here… let me tell you, you are a good person you are, and that is why i grace you now with my big crucifix cock, here, feel it, want it…? i'll shove it up there and cauterize your insides, all those old wounds, all those unhealed scars, or do you want me to rip it all up, tear up your insides until you shit your soul out your arsehole… tell me. i whisper in your ear now, i tell you you did wrong, you should have raped her nightly, Selena, moon to your earth, raped her nightly and spawned an array of starchildren, raped them too for all your worth, that is the measure of a man, one who knows how to take, take it all, take everything. that is a man. and you are a man. you are my man. let me be your father and fuck you til your break. let me be your brother and take the shirt off your back. let me be your mother and crawl inside me. let me be your child and eat your insides. i am all things. in all things am i, the umbra and the penumbra, the sun that casts no shadow. see me and know me not at your peril. but wait—we have forgotten the quintessence. look—see the boy, behold the child…that is you. *you.* do you, the man, accept the child? or do you, the man, reject him? this child spurned by cuntmother and fatherbastard, this cuntchild, little cuntfucker, look at the poor cuntfucker weep. you, this? reject him. reject him and be the man. be the man and not cuntchild. let's rape cuntchild both of us, i'll tear his insides and you desecrate his heart, punch a hole in his chest and fuck his heart til it bursts. let us destroy together. be with me. be mine. i am the fire, the mind fire, i will eat destroy mind eat your mind destroy YOUR FUCKING MIND MINDFIRE MINDFIRE CUNTFUC KFROMTHEINSIDEOUTPLUNDERYOURSOUL-CUNTBO ILYOURSOULPUNCTUREYOUWITHFUCKINGEMPTINE SS —

— —

— —

    'Vangelis?'

Vangelis felt someone shake him. Then a hand on his face, and another. Two hands traveled over the rough contours of his cheeks, seeking familiarity.

'Is it you?' a voice whispered.

He opened his eyes and saw his mother. Thrashing out in horror, he struck her. The woman fell back with a cry. Vangelis turned to crawl away, but she put a hand on his shoulder.

'It's me… it's only me…'

He felt the warmth of her touch and turned, and looked up at her again.

The woman wore a rag over her eyes. Her cheeks were bloodied. But he knew her, knew the nose and the sad countenance of her mouth.

'Celeste?'

'I found you.'

She knelt in front of him, a lost penitent. Her face contorted as she fought the urge to sob, though no tears came from beneath the bloodied rag that covered her eyes.

'What happened to you?' he croaked hoarsely.

Her body crumbled, as if her soul had just relived some terrible suffering. 'Birds ate out my eyes.' She shook with a fresh terror.

Vangelis, remembering in that moment his own horror, clutched desperately at his genitals. He found them intact.

'It's not real,' he whispered. 'None of it is real. We're in a programmed reality right now. This is not real.'

'It feels real,' Celeste said, her body wracked with grief.

Vangelis, whether overcome by Celeste's afflictions, or assaulted by his own suffering, put his head in his hands and began to weep. Soon his body was shaking. He fell forward until his head was in Celeste's lap. She put a hand on his head and they wept together, the two of them cut like a sculpture honed from the mind of some tortured, abandoned soul.

They sat like that for a long time. When their tears were spent, Vangelis raised himself up, wiped his face, and sat for a long moment, silent in his shame. Then he turned to the disfigured woman beside him.

'We have to go.'

She looked defeated. 'Go where?'

'I don't know. We need to find a way out. If Saleh can penetrate to the main servers Verne can find a way to break us out of here. We just gotta hope they can do it in time. I think we need to stay on our feet.'

'There's no corner of this place they can't find us.' Celeste raised her head as if hearing some distant noise.

'Well, let's not make it easy for them.'

'We're in Hell, aren't we?'

Vangelis nodded. Then he took her hand. 'I think that's where we are, yes. At least some psychopath's idea of what Hell is.'

'Your company made this.'

'Yes.'

She held out a hand. He put his arm around her and together they stood.

'You're going to have to guide me,' she said.

'That's alright. We'll go slowly.'

'Where are we right now?'

Vangelis paused to look around him. 'We're in a room. It has burgundy walls, no windows, no furniture. One door. There's a painting on one wall.'

'What's the painting?'

'It's just... black. Black oil.'

'Is the door locked?'

'Let's find out.'

Vangelis led Celeste to the door. He put a hand on the handle and turned. The door opened. Vangelis looked out to find a corridor on the other side, seemingly empty, brightly lit and with deep blue walls. A heavy silence hung in the air.

'What is it?' Celeste tightened her grip on his arm.

'It's a corridor.'

'I don't hear anything.'

'Neither do I. It's fucking unsettling.'

He stepped out, Celeste going after him. As soon as her feet were over the threshold, the door shut with a deep hollow echo. The noise of it shook them.

'What do we do now?'

Vangelis didn't answer. He looked up and down the corridor. A series of equally spaced doors led away in either direction, but he was reluctant to try any of them. His experiences so far had taught him only one thing: there was nothing good in this place. He felt Celeste's hand tighten on his arm.

He placed his hand on hers.

'We just gotta move. I don't know where. Maybe our guts will guide us.'

'I'll follow.'

Vangelis turned right and walked slowly with Celeste on his arm. The cavernous silence of the place seemed to eat up their desire to communicate, as if the silence itself was an absence into which all activity was drawn to its demise. Soon Vangelis felt like he was wading through heavy air; the silence seemed to take on a thickness he had to labor to penetrate.

A sound reached him through the treacle-like suffocation.

He turned his head. 'Huh?'

Celeste stopped walking. 'I said there are doors.'

Vangelis looked around him. 'Yes. There are.'

Celeste reached out a hand. 'I can feel them. I can feel the weight of whatever's behind them.' She pointed. 'That one…'

'You want me to open it?'

'I need to know what's inside.'

Vangelis took a meditative breath. 'I'm not sure that's a good idea. Especially if you can *feel* whatever's behind that door.'

'We can't just walk forever. We have to go through one. This one – there's something dark inside but it's not dangerous. It won't hurt us. Not if we don't succumb to it.'

'Fuck. I don't know…'

She squeezed his arm. 'Trust me.'

He sighed. 'Alright.'

Slipping from her grip, he moved to the door. 'You sure?'

She nodded.

He turned the handle and pushed it open, only a crack at first. Glancing through the gap in the door, he saw only darkness.

'You see anything?' Celeste whispered.

Vangelis opened the door further until the light from the corridor illuminated the room. The room was in darkness, a darkness so profound that the floor, walls and ceiling could not be discerned with clarity. In the middle of the room, almost as if it was floating there, was a porcelain toilet.

'What is it?'

'It's the toilet.'

'What?'

'It's the toilet. Hell's toilet.' He almost grinned.

'No… there's something else. I feel it… it's like it's sucking in all the energy of the universe… like it's pouring into it and turning into dark energy.'

'I feel it too.'

Vangelis felt its pull. Felt the desire, the compulsion, to walk toward it and let himself be sucked into dark oblivion.

Vangelis attempted a joke. 'So, I guess if I really needed to go, I'd just have to hold it, right?'

'You can't go into that room.'

He shuddered. 'Yeah. I know.'

Then something changed. Both of them felt it. Like the direction of the energy slowed, imperceptibly at first, then more quickly, until it drew to a stop altogether. There was a moment of great stillness. Then the flow began again, only this time the energy was coming out of the toilet, first a trickle, and with it vague, unsubstantial orbs of light that seemed to contain within them undulating contortions of dark matter. Then it came faster, until the roar of it began to overwhelm the two of them.

'Close it!' Celeste shouted.

As he pulled the door, Vangelis thought he saw a great black form emerge from the toilet, a being with eyes of silver that harbored more hate than is contained in a thousand humans, and as the door slammed shut, little dark whisps of smoke caught in the jamb. A narrow escape from something so dark as to be unfathomable.

Celeste and Vangelis felt a terrible dread creep up their spines.

'I thought you said it couldn't hurt us?'

Celeste shook her head. 'It changed. The room changed.'

Vangelis nodded.

'Nothing in here is what it seems.'

Vangelis took her arm gently. 'Come on. Let's go.'

Celeste let herself be led. After a few moments of silence, she said, 'I don't know what to do to get out of here.'

'That's alright. Let's just stick together. We'll figure something out.' After a pause, he added, 'Or maybe Saleh will figure it out for us.'

Celeste let an audible moan escape her lips. 'I hope he's alright.'

'He's a smart kid. Good instincts. He'll make it.'

The blue of the corridor seemed to undulate from a deep cerulean to a dark midnight; the far reaches in either direction were pitch black. The silence was interrupted by what sounded like the rattling tumbler of a lock.

They both stopped.

Celeste's fingers tensed on Vangelis's arm. 'Did you hear that?'

'Yes.'

They stood in silence, still, poised for the noise to sound again. It came.

'I can't place it. Where's it coming from?' Celeste turned to look behind her.

'I don't know. It's like it's everywhere.'

It sounded again.

'That way.' Vangelis began to pull Celeste back the way they'd come.

She stood her ground. 'No.' She pointed forward. 'It's that way.'

'I don't think so…'

'I'm sure.'

Vangelis looked up and down the corridor. 'We can't go two ways.'

'There's only one way.' Celeste raised a hand to point, and as she did, they heard the key in the lock rattle louder. Right beside them. They turned to the door next to them, stepping back and bracing themselves.

When the door opened, a small child in a shabby nightdress stood there, still on tiptoes as she pulled the door handle. A little girl clutching a tattered-looking ragdoll. The child let the door swing open and stepped back.She looked like a poor creature who'd spent years locked in a basement or an attic. But when she spoke, her words were clear and calm.

She pointed back into the room. 'You can see him now.'

Celeste, her maternal instincts kindled at the sound of the young voice, stepped forward. 'Who?' She went to get down onto her hunkers to meet the source of the childish voice, but Vangelis put a cautious hand on her shoulder.

'Saleh.'

Celeste gasped. 'He's here?'

The child nodded.

Vangelis stepped forward and put two hands on Celeste's shoulders, as if afraid she might dash off after the child.

'Celeste… we need to be careful.'

She turned her unseeing face to him. 'This child has been sent to help us.'

'How do you know?'

'I can feel it.' She turned back to the child and held out a hand. 'Take us to him.' When Celeste sensed Vangelis's hesitation, she turned to him. 'Trust me.'

He nodded. He came up behind her as she followed the strange urchin into the room. Once inside, the door closed. Vangelis glanced at it with suspicion.

'This way,' the child said, taking Celeste's hand.

The room was sparse, the walls bare. A small cot bed lay

against one wall and a child-sized table and chair against another. On the table was a mannikin head with a dark-haired wig. The lips were painted garishly and the cheeks smudged with rouge. Makeup was scattered over the table. Vangelis eyed the bust with a gnawing in his gut as they passed.

The child led Celeste to another door at the back of the room and passed through, stopping to close the door when they were all inside. The room was bathed in a rose light, the source of which was an aquarium-like window that spanned the back wall of the room. What was on the other side wasn't water, but it undulated with its own density. Celeste's head turned this way and that, searching with her all her working senses for Saleh.

'Where is he?' she uttered, grasping that he was not in the room with them.

The child took Celeste by one hand, Vangelis the other, and led them toward the window. As they drew nearer the room darkened but the rose light grew in intensity.

'Do you see anything?' Celeste whispered.

'Nothing,' Vangelis replied. He looked down at the child.

The child raised a finger to point through the glass. 'Look. We are coming.'

5

Saleh stood frozen, the whites of his eyes stark in the red light. He looked at the child in front of him, as if this diminutive, lost-looking innocent could deliver him from the terror now hunting him.

'W-What is it?' he stammered. 'What's coming?'

He heard the rapid tap of small feet on the steel floor; perhaps on the walls and ceiling too. Industrious and efficient sounding. Purposeful. Aimed right in his direction.

He turned back around. 'What is—?'

The child was gone. Saleh spun to scan every direction, but the girl was nowhere to be seen. The realization that he was alone hit him like a brick. Compelled to it, he ran. Away from that which pursued him.

Saleh ran blindly around corners. The server stacks towering above seemed to close in on him. Moments they appeared like the buildings of his home city: the financial district at night, as he was less accustomed to seeing it – from the ground, not from the roofs above where he preferred to be.

Screeching reached his ears from the creatures in pursuit. The sound was like the tearing of metal. It seemed to pull at his insides, filling him with cold terror.

Bolting around corners he went, now this way, now that,

the heat increasing, the blood pumping around his young body and the thud of his heart in his ears until the room itself seemed to pulse with the violence of it, he fled unknowing through that maze with only his bare instinct to guide him. A particularly violent screech caused him to look up; on the roof above, he thought he caught sight of one of his hunters, shaped like an enormous vile spider but with a gait that seemed mechanical, two glowing red orbs at the head, sinister eyes filled with a cold, calculating, unwavering menace; Saleh heard it screech again then saw the thing leap. He cried out and dashed around a corner and out of the thing's grasp. He thought he felt a tugging at his jacket – *his imagination?* – didn't wait to find out, kept on running, running, until, feeling like his heart would burst out of his chest, he turned a corner and found himself in front of a large ectoplasm-like membrane that ran from floor to ceiling. He came skidding to a halt. With no time to process what it was, whether it could hurt or harm him, and with the creature bearing down at his back, a screeching right above him, he took a single glance over his shoulder then leapt at the wall, puncturing the filmy skin like a fist into a still-warm carcass. He hit the floor on the other side, the skin closing up where he'd cleaved through. The creature, his pursuer, screeched on the other side of the membrane but did not follow. Saleh saw it through the thin ectoplasmic wall, its legs scrambling over the membrane in an attempt to pass. He saw the shadow of another. And another. There must have been half a dozen, scratching all over and trying to penetrate. Saleh slid back on the floor, not taking his eyes off the membrane and the shadow of his hunters.

He was safe, it seemed. For now.

He raised a hand to his face then ran fingers through his hair. He was covered in a sticky mucus, a residue from his passing through the membrane. He wiped it from his face and flicked it off. The rest of it, he left be. He stood up and looked around.

From what he could see, the skin he'd passed through

formed an enclosure on four sides and above. It seemed he was in some kind of central chamber. As long as it kept out his pursuers, he figured he had time to look around and see just where he was and how he might get out. Or perhaps find something pertinent to his reason for being there.

The area looked like some kind of control room; he'd watched a movie once about a nuclear disaster, and the scene in the control room as things were going bad was something like what he was looking at now. It looked like that, only a place that had not been in operation for a long time. There were lots of computers and panels and things, but nothing seemed to be in working order. Moss grew over much of the machinery, and dewy web-like stuff grew in corners. Buttons were caked with dust and rust bedecked the panels. It was a place suspended in time. What Saleh was doing there, he had no idea. But he had to find a way out.

He stopped in front of a desk where there was an old primitive phone-type thing. He knew what it was because his dad had once taken him to a heritage museum where they had loads of stuff from the old days. He'd seen one of these old receivers and his dad had put it to his son's ear and told him to make like he was making a call, and Saleh pretended he was talking to Bolted Dan, who was a character from his favorite TV show and someone he'd always dreamed of meeting. He thought of that moment now as he picked up the black receiver and put it to his ear, thinking he could hear a low drumming sound but was probably just the sound of his heart which was still thrumming too fast.

'*Control?*' he said, softly so his hunters might not hear him. Too loud still, for the pattering of feet outside the command room picked up and became frantic.

Saleh put down the receiver.

He looked to the ceiling; the mechanical legs of one of his pursuers pattered over the protective membrane. He felt vulnerable. What if the membrane ripped and they all poured through? They would cut him to pieces in seconds.

Saleh moved between each station as silently as he could, looking for some, any, activity. All the screens appeared dead. He tapped a few buttons on each keyboard but to no avail. He sighed, and looked around him in desperation.

He sat down at the central terminal. It was a long desk with a single keyboard and three monitors. On either side of the monitors was an array of darkened lights, each labeled in a language Saleh could not decipher. He closed his eyes, trying to picture the scene as it had been when it was fully operational, the tremendous power that could be exercised over a whole technological kingdom, all from this single seat. He placed his two hands on the desk and took a breath. He was master. He was the operator. He was the one who could command this complex machinery and bend it to his will. When he opened his eyes, his narrowed gaze alighted on a plug below the left monitor. At the same time, he felt an itching in his wrist. He reached out and pulled the mono-jack plug from its receptor. It had a fine jack, not quite needle sharp but less than a millimeter wide and over an inch long. He looked at his wrist. He knew what he had to do. He brought it close to his skin, pressed it into his wrist but stopped short of breaking the skin. He didn't like pain – who did? But there was no mistaking it – this is what he had to do. He just knew. Gritting his teeth, he pushed the jack through the skin, right into his vein.

He felt a tingle run up the veins of his arm, an itch that begged to be scratched at with his fingernails. He looked down at the jack, resisting the temptation to rip it out.

He noticed a flicker on the central monitor in front of him. Slowly, a word appeared there letter by letter:

'F…U…S…E'

After a second's pause, Saleh reached forward and began to punch the keys with a single finger:

'B…R…I…D…G…E'

A bright explosion lit up the synapses of his brain for a split second, causing his body to bolt as if he'd just been shocked.

Something flowed through him. And while it wasn't exactly pleasant, it wasn't like he wanted it to stop. It was as if there were a legion of minuscule insects crawling through his veins carrying with them whole worlds of knowledge. Not like he was filling up with it, but if he wanted to, he knew he could access it. It was there, just waiting for him to reach out and take it, just like plucking a book from a library shelf. So much of it, it threatened to overwhelm him.

He closed his eyes and focused his mind, imagining himself in a vast library filled floor to ceiling with books. The more he focused, the more fixed and concrete the library became in his mind. He'd never been in one, and the library he conjured up was drawn solely from images he'd seen in movies: two floors supported by classical columns and pointed arches, and with a vaulted ceiling; the main floor filled with large oak tables with individual reading lamps on each, the lamps illuminated with a soft yellow light; here and there, nooks and crannies where the private reader might escape for a time from the clamor of the city; and hanging from the ceiling, chandeliers which cast an incarnadine glow over the austere room. There was no librarian and no one else there, just him and this vast athenaeum of knowledge and information.

Now standing in this conjured library, Saleh looked at the ceiling in awe. He turned to take in the cavernous nature of the place which seemed vaster than a football field.

He focused on the filled shelves. As he did, he felt an excitement in his body, as if the apparatus that worked through him and coursed through his veins was alert to the possibility of knowledge and its acquirement. Saleh moved between the tables toward the nearest shelf. Approaching it, he saw the shelf was marked 'THEATER'. He plucked the closest book from its resting place and opened it; without warning it was as if the atoms of his body began to vibrate with the accumulation of strange and hitherto unknown things, as his limbs began to muster new energies and his mind filled with strange words like 'Kabuki' and 'Brecht' and

'Pathos' and 'Denouement'. Overwhelmed by the onrush of new sensations, and the violent flush it caused in his mind and body, he slammed the book shut. His breath coming fast, he replaced the book on the shelf.

Saleh recalled why he was here. Recalled his training. Remembered the reason he'd joined with Celeste and Eric and Verne, and the reason he was in this very room: his best friend was dead. *Killed*. Killed by the people who'd built the software through which he was now being pursued. He had to get what he came for. Had to retrieve the evidence and get out. Otherwise he might be trapped here forever.

Saleh turned to look over his shoulder at the upper floor. That's where he had to go. Seized with a sudden sense of urgency, he turned and began to run, reaching the stairs and leaping up them two at a time until he was at the top. Hurrying down the hall, he made his way past row upon row of books stacked to the ceiling, right to the end where, under the main apse of the building, a purpose-built fortified room sat under the expansive glass panels of the ceiling. The door was open. Above it, the sign said 'SPECIAL COLLECTIONS'. Saleh paused, looking up at the sign and wondering what it meant. But he had a good idea what it meant. This is where all the sensitive stuff was. The stuff they were after. The stuff Eric and Verne and the others needed to help bring down Vathos.

Saleh stepped across the threshold, half-expecting some alarm system to begin ringing. But he'd already passed through the security systems and was inside the core. Now all he had to do was grab the information he needed and get the hell out.

A sudden noise in his head startled him.

—Saleh…

'Verne?' The boy put a hand to his ear and looked upward. 'Is that you, Verne? Can you hear me?'

The noise crackled out only to come back more vaguely.

—…inside the serv…looking for 'espionage'…'subv—

'Verne? You're breaking up, I can't hear you...'
—'Infiltration'...

Saleh heard that word very clearly.

'Verne? Verne!'

So close... yet separated by worlds. Saleh thought Verne might be able to see where Saleh was, what he was doing, and could be trying to communicate directions to him. But the connection was too unstable.

Saleh looked around the room, his eyes alighting on one word beneath a shelf stacked with files: 'INFILTRATION'. And another: 'SUBVERSION'.

This is what he was here for. Saleh moved to the shelf and lifted files from the first, planted them atop a pile from the second shelf, then lifted the lot and put them on the table at the center of the room. He sat down and took a file from the top of the pile and opened it. Immediately the 'apparatus' sparked into life, the circuitry that flowed through his body coming alive with forbidden knowledge. He oscillated with it, and when he'd worked his way through the first file he closed it and lifted the next. Like this he worked his way through the whole array until, closing the last one, he slumped into the chair with an elated exhaustion.

Processing all the information he'd just consumed, his eyes darkened. What terrible things he had come to know. What terrible, terrible things. This world he had stumbled into, this awful terrible life he lived... he'd rather not learned anything of it, not learned of it at all. He realized he was now filled with a knowledge he might never rid himself of.

He got up from the chair. He looked to the door, keen to get out of here, but he remembered he had one more piece of information to acquire. Impatient now, he looked around the room, seeing a dusty set of drawers that seemed to draw his eye. He went over to it and opened it, and began pushing around the contents, not seeing the thing he searched for. Likewise he checked the middle drawer, and finally the bottom. It was at the back of the bottom drawer where he seemed to chance upon the thing he sought, a file with the name 'ZERVAS'.

Quickly, he opened it and scanned through it, his eyes taking in schedules and photographs and lists and histories, until, reaching the last page, he snapped it shut and let it drop back in the open drawer. His head fell. This was a burden no child should have to bear.

He'd seen enough. Now it was time to go. To make his escape. To get out with the acquired information, preferably alive.

Saleh hurried to the door, stopping in the doorway to look back around the room. So much hidden knowledge, so much compromising information. Things herein that could break worlds. Had he seen enough? Had he collected sufficient kompromat? Or could he ingest still more?

No. It was enough. He hadn't the stomach for more.

He stepped outside. No sooner had he crossed the threshold than the lights went down. An alarm sounded, high and violent in its intensity. Saleh froze, then, gripped by the desire to be gone, put his hand on the banister. With barely a second thought, he launched himself over the banister.

He came to, seated at the dusty control panel but with the alarm still sounding. Looking down at his arm he saw the needle still embedded there. He took hold of it and extracted it from his skin. A beeping sounded from the panel in front of him as he dropped the needle, and an LED light came on in a tiny compartment right above the keyboard. Saleh reached over and lifted the glass cover; a small panel slid open to reveal a MicroSD card. Saleh picked it up. This was it – all his illicit knowledge. He looked at it briefly; not knowing what else to do, he put it in his mouth and swallowed.

Hearing a tearing sound behind him, fear gripped him. He turned. A mechanical leg pierced through the membrane protecting him from his hunters. Dozens of busy limbs poked the filmy skin, slicing through into the protective womb within. He was cornered.

Saleh turned and darted behind the console, scanning 360 degrees with his eyes on the lookout for some exit. At the back, beneath one of the consoles touching the membrane, an arm poked through, followed by a body. But this was no spider. It was the child, the same little girl who'd helped him before. Looking as helpless as ever, she passed through the membrane and stood up, and held out a hand to Saleh.

'We should go now,' she said in her pitiful child's voice.

Saleh wasted no time. He hurried over to her, and ducked under the console after her as she disappeared back through the membrane.

He followed her through a small, tight tunnel on his hands and knees. It was dark. As they went, he had only the sound of shuffling in front of him to follow.

After a long time crawling in the darkness, they reached the end.

He emerged in a long dark room, at one end of it a rose-tinted window. He stood looking at the strangeness of it, only turning away his eyes to look down at the child as she slipped her small hand into his. She beckoned him forward.

She led him through the empty room toward the rose window. As they neared, figures began to materialize on the other side: two adult figures, a child too. The closer they got, the clearer the figures became. When he was only feet from the window, Saleh saw who they were.

Celeste and Vangelis. With them, the same young girl who now held his hand. Vangelis shouted his name; Celeste put a hand against the window.

'Celeste...' Saleh looked from the woman to the young child next to him. 'Celeste... that's Celeste!'

Celeste's eyes were covered with a rag. She was reaching out to him. He threw himself forward, placing a hand into the imprint of hers.

'I got it,' Saleh cried. 'I got it!'

Celeste nodded, smiled. Her face contorted as if she was crying.

'I got it,' Saleh whispered, relieved he'd found his friends again. Yet separated by the rose window, he felt as far from them as he'd ever been.

6

Vangelis glanced at Celeste, then looked down at the child standing between them. He turned back to the window to gaze through it at the boy, who stood staring back at them, the same decrepit girl-child next to him. Celeste, hand on the glass, turned to look at him.

'What's happening? Is it really him?'

Vangelis looked pointedly at Saleh as he spoke. 'Yes.'

'Why is he here? Why can we not reach him?'

Vangelis shook his head. 'I don't know. There must be some bleeding of the programs. The program we're in was built on the Vathos servers, so they must be linked in some way. A back door or something.'

'So he just found his way into this terrible place?'

'Or maybe he was led.' Vangelis looked down for the child who'd brought them here. The child was gone. He lifted his head to look through the mirror – the child with Saleh had also disappeared. Vangelis looked around the room frantically.

'Little shit…'

Celeste looked up. 'What… what is it?'

'The child… she's gone.'

Celeste nodded. 'She did what she had to do.'

'Yeah… led us into this dead end.'

Vangelis looked at Saleh. He'd just noticed the absence of

the girl and was looking around the room distractedly.

'How do we get to him?' Celeste said, desperation in her voice.

Vangelis's face tautened into a grim mask. 'I'm not sure we can.'

'We have to try.'

Vangelis nodded. As he did, he saw a shadow materialize behind the boy. Celeste didn't see it, but she felt Vangelis shudder.

She froze. 'Is something there?'

Vangelis's voice dropped to a whisper. 'On the other side of the window…'

'With Saleh?'

Vangelis didn't answer. He stared fixedly at the shadow that was festering, growing, at the boy's back. As it drew nearer, it took on a shiny appearance, the figure of a man. A man heavy with the weight of souls.

Vangelis saw Celeste begin to shrink at the man's energy.

'God help us… what is it?' she whispered. 'I can see it. I can see its… shadow.'

The figure behind Saleh became clear now: a heavy-set man in a gaudy silver suit, his face full yet somehow hollowed out, dark; a tattoo crawled up from his open shirt and wound around his neck, and his fingers were bedecked with gold rings. His eyes were black, black as the void night. He slid an arm around Saleh's shoulder. His tongue flicked out over his lower lip and hung there grossly for a second. Vangelis felt terror climb his spine. Celeste beat the window with her palms.

'You leave him be… you hear me, you leave him be!'

Vangelis put an arm around her. To his dismay, he watched as Saleh slid a hand onto the man's arm affectionately and looked up at him with warmth in his eyes.

'What's he doing?' Celeste cried.

'His mind must be poisoned,' Vangelis said. 'He's not himself.'

Catching him unawares, the man in the silver suit glanced up from the boy to look Vangelis in the eye. Vangelis felt as if a black finger was digging into his chest trying to pierce his heart. He clutched his breast.

He took a hold of Celeste's arm. 'Come on… we have to go. We have to get out of here.'

Celeste pulled away. 'We can't leave him. We can't leave him there.'

The man in the silver suit looked down at Saleh. Then he backed away, taking the child with him. He cast a final dark smirk at Vangelis and Celeste as he dematerialized into the shadows from which he'd come.

'He wants us to follow. He's goading us.' Vangelis pulled Celeste gently from the window. 'Come on… we'll find him. We'll get him back.'

Celeste reached a hand out to the window as Vangelis pulled her away, her fingers grasping at thin air.

They walked in pale darkness for a long time, Vangelis leading the unseeing Celeste, down corridors and through caverns, over rocks, alongside a bleeding river, times on their feet and times on their hands and knees, led the while by an unerring unspoken belief, or perhaps desperation, that something wanted them to find the boy, that something was guiding them, ensuring yet another innocent life would not be lost to this hellscape.

Having stumbled in the dark for longer than they knew, and finding themselves on a long, endless bridge of sorts, soon they came upon a stranger shuffling in the darkness ahead of them.

Vangelis stopped.

'What is it?' Celeste whispered.

'There's someone there, up in front.'

'What are they doing?'

'Just walking.' He paused. 'Not even walking. He's dragging himself along.'

'Is he dangerous?'

'I don't think so. Come on.'

Vangelis led Celeste onward until they were almost walking alongside the figure. Vangelis looked at the man; the man did not lift his gaze. He walked on, visage slung low. Vangelis was horrified to see no face there; no face that was recognizably human. There was a 'face', but without features. Eyes of a sort peered from two black holes in the mask, but otherwise the face resembled some hollowed-out disk. A blank nothingness.

Celeste tugged at Vangelis's arm. 'What is it?'

'I have no idea.' Vangelis raised his voice to holler at the creature. 'Hey… hey you…'

It did not respond, did not even acknowledge the words.

He pulled Celeste further away from the creature. 'It's a dead thing.'

Vangelis put an arm around Celeste and propelled her on, almost tripping when he sensed another of these creatures come up behind them. Another appeared at their side.

'Where are they coming from?'

Celeste shuddered. 'Where are they going is the real question.' She paused. 'And where are we going.'

Soon they were surrounded by these walking dead. They marched in unison, unseeing and unthinking, across the bridge over the bleeding river. On the other side, Vangelis saw at last a glow emanating from what seemed the domed entrance to a cave of sorts. Celeste, following silently, stopped, her grip on Vangelis's arm tightening.

'I feel something… what do you see?'

Vangelis shook his head. 'Some kind of big room up ahead. There's a fire burning in it. Looks like flames flickering.'

'I'm not sure we want to go there.'

Vangelis looked around at the army of souls marching unified toward their common fate.

'I don't think we have a choice.' He looked over his shoulder. The souls marching across the bridge were so thick they couldn't beat their way back if they wanted to. They were propelled forward regardless of will or intention. They let themselves be carried over the bridge to the entrance to the cave in which a vast fire glowed.

As they neared the domed entrance, Vangelis looked up to see a horned symbol cut into the rock, like a circle with a crowned half-moon. He didn't know what it meant, but he was sure he'd seen the same symbol on Roche's wall. He wondered if he'd ever see her again. Ever finish his back-piece. Maybe he'd never see it brought to completion.

They were herded through the entrance with all the lost souls into a vast cavern of sorts. The cavern resembled a large quarry, with a central bowl ringed by a rising spiral that ran up the walls of the cavern into the darkness beyond. The central bowl was filled with a lake of churning fire. Vangelis felt the heat of it assault his face. The dead souls with whom they'd entered the great cavern were circling the lake of fire, each of them in turn stopping to face it. One by one, their faces lifted from the ground to stare at some unseen thing above their heads.

A sense of dread assailed Vangelis and Celeste.

'I don't like it…' Vangelis whispered.

Celeste moved closer to him. 'Neither do I. And I can't even see what's happening.'

Vangelis looked around the cavern. The trapped souls had taken up a bizarre formation around the lake of fire, as if preparing for some ghastly ritual. He raised his eyes to follow the line of the spiral path that led into the vaulted ceiling of the cavern, to see if it might lead to some escape. The thought of climbing it filled him with dread.

As he gazed upward, from the corner of his eye he saw flickering lights several circuits of the spiral up the wall. Two torches, which appeared to flank a figure seated in a chair. He felt the figure was watching them. For a moment, he couldn't tear his eye away from the figure. Then something occurred around them.

It started as a hum. Something emanating from the dead

souls. It began softly, growing in intensity as a single figure from among their number made its way toward the edge of the lake of fire.

'I don't like this,' Celeste whispered. 'We need to go.'

The figure stopped at the edge of the lake, its terrible void face still raised. Vangelis thought it was raised to the sinister figure sitting above. The hum around them rose in pitch and intensity, all the souls screeching in unison. Celeste put her hands to her ears. A terrible furor arose, a scream which emanated from the faces of the dead, a scream torn from their empty souls, their hollowed-out faces acting as a kind of amplifier for this god-awful uproar. It pierced Vangelis to his very center. As the scream rose to fever pitch, the figure by the side of the lake flung himself into the flames and disappeared with a burning flash of flame.

Horrified, Vangelis put an arm around Celeste and pushed her through these terrible dead things, pushing her out of the cacophony to somewhere they might find reprieve.

When they were out of the circle of souls, Vangelis guided Celeste into a hollow in the rock and sat her down. The creatures behind them still screamed hell.

Vangelis removed the hands that covered Celeste's ears.

'I'm going up there,' he shouted, pointing up in the vague direction of the seated figure. 'Stay here and don't move. I won't be long.'

Celeste shook her head vigorously. 'No… don't leave me.'

He took her face in his hands. 'Just stay put. Cover your ears and don't move.'

Despite the despair on her face and the appeal rising in her throat, Vangelis turned and hurried to the bottom of the spiral path. He stopped, took a look at the winding route that led to the man in the chair. Then he started running.

Immediately he was hit by a searing wind that burned red hot against his face. He raised his arms to protect himself and ran, propelling himself against the ripping gusts that tore against him, threatening to rip the shirt from his back and the skin from his torso. He stumbled, striking his knees on the rough rock, getting back up and immediately throwing himself into the wind, slowing to look about him to gauge the height and the distance he'd covered but seeing nothing; he plowed on, lips burning in the dry lacerating whip of the wind. It was murderous, and it was endless. After an interminable time in which the will to go on was sapped from him like resin from a wizened tree, with an abruptness that sounded like a sonic boom the wind stopped, in its place a vacuum of silence. Vangelis fell to the floor on his face and lay prone and unmoving, his limbs numb. He lay there, the sound of the silence suspending him in a kind of limbic nullity.

It was the feeling of two claw-like extremities taking him under the arms that caused him to raise his head. He felt himself lifted and carried a short distance then dropped on the ground roughly. When he raised his head, he beheld something terrible.

Before him in a great throne of stone sat a lord of the dead: pale were his robes and white his skin, white and taut over his bones like the bleached carcasses of the desert, and his face a puckered and drawn death mask with lips like parchment and eyes two suck-holes into which souls were plucked from the endless parade of dead. Eternal was his dominion and his dominion was the oblivion of the spirit. To look upon him was to glimpse, over eons and eternities, the vast unconquerable nothingness that was the dearth of all being.

To only look upon this death angel Vangelis felt the spirit leave him and he lowered his eyes and sunk to the floor. The death angel was flanked by two demons, thin red-skinned figures that held themselves like vultures on the island of the dead, faces like beaks sated on the black blood of the condemned. No sound came from the three figures; their silence was like the immense torrent of endless night.

And then, with a vast sucking of air, the death angel spoke.

'Two came, and yet you are one.' His voice was dead as the stones around him.

Vangelis fought the dread weariness that assailed him. 'The other is below. She is blind.'

'All are blind here.'

Recalling the scores of dead below, Vangelis acceded with a nod. He mustered his will and raised his face to the death angel. A searing pain filled his head when he met the black eyes.

'What do you want?'

'I want to see him. I want the boy back.'

The death angel raised a hand and extended a dire finger. 'All who would see him must go there.'

Vangelis didn't have to look – he knew the angel indicated the lake of fire.

He shouted. 'I don't belong here! This is not my place. This is not her place. Let us leave with the boy!'

A cutting electricity tore through his veins and caused his body to spasm. His face contorted like that of a man in the electric chair. When the pain released him, he let out an animal wail. Putting a hand on the stone ground, he pushed himself up onto his knees and then to his feet, the weight of centuries on his shoulder.

'I demand to leave!'

A hot scream emanated from the death angel, which burned Vangelis's face. The two demons flew at him like the arrows of hell, snatching him by the arms and propelling him off the cliff face. Vangelis felt the terror of the fall, an acceleration, then the bone-breaking smash of his body on the stone below. The air was driven from his body piston-like and he felt the blood rush to his head. It came to him then that he was only moments from dying.

He looked up to see Celeste standing over him. He raised a hand and she took it, and he attempted to stand up.

'Don't move,' she said, the hollow scream of the dead souls once again echoing around them.

He insisted. He had no choice. Broken bones and all, he took hold of Celeste's shoulder and pulled himself up, and despite her protests she let him haul himself to his feet, mangled and wobbling but upright. He put an arm around her neck.

'You'll forgive me for this, I promise.'

Celeste felt his grip on her tighten. 'Forgive you for what?'

Gripping her and not letting go, Vangelis surged forward with the last strength he could raise, dragging her with him to the pit of fire.

The scream of the dead souls reached a crescendo, and that scream seemed to open the gates of Hell.

Celeste screamed with them.

○

I am the other son, the spurned seed.
The forgotten, the castaway.
My father, fled; my whore mother lost to a myriad men.
Prodigal, yet I returned not to the house I incinerated.

I eat scripture and regurgitate stone,
castigate the rank heresy of the just.
I am the shadow that strangulates,
the umbra and penumbra my rhyolitic husk;
fire the means by which I cleanse and
incise the rank corruption from their core.

Burn, I say they shall burn.
Cleansed in the flames which consume my house,
they shall enter only by absolution.

This is the last, this is the last.
Enter here and sin no more.
I will cut the corruption from your soul
For I am the fire, the burning coal.
I rise before you, a black sun
o'er a dark meadow.
Burn, and become an imprint of ash, ash cast
eternal in the book of shadows.

7

Ordained in the fires of hell and anointed in torment, atoms cleaved clean one from the other, flung, a million explosions, the body dispersed and the mind eviscerated. A momentary torment yet without cease. Infinite torture.

Reconstituted. Reborn.

Now in a vast spherical room that shines like buffed chrome. No corners, no doors.

In the center, a table. In front of them, the man in the silver suit. Two hands on the table. Eyes on them. Standing next to him at his shoulder, Saleh.

Vangelis and Celeste, purged in the fire, sat next to each other on the other side of the table. Vangelis glanced at Celeste. She no longer wore the rag around her head; where her eyes once were, were two gaping holes. He reached over and put a hand on her wrist. She responded by putting a hand on his.

Vangelis turned his face to the man in the silver suit. Terrible he was to behold. Not big, or monstrous, but a man devoid of all humanity, an emptiness which threatened to drown those sitting before him.

Saleh stood unmoving and obedient next to him. He wasn't uncomfortable, or afraid, but strangely contented.

'What have you done to him?' Vangelis said, his voice more strained than he wished it to be.

The man looked at Vangelis. After a long moment he spoke.

'Wouldn't you prefer not to have eyes?' He glanced at Celeste. 'She looks more resigned than you.'

'I would prefer to leave this place,' Vangelis said.

'Would you.' The man nodded. Without taking his eyes off Vangelis, he reached into his jacket and took out a silver cigarette case and a lighter. He opened the case and took out a cigarette and put it between his lips, then lit it, all in a detached manner, then took the cigarette between his thumb and forefinger and exhaled. 'Of course you would. No one chooses this place, do they?'

Celeste reached out with her right hand and gripped the edge of the table. 'We just want the boy.' She turned her head to Saleh. 'Saleh? Are you okay? Talk to me, tell me something…'

Saleh looked at the man in the silver suit. He nodded.

'I'm fine.' Saleh smiled.

'You've poisoned him.' Celeste began to stand up, but Vangelis restrained her with a hand. The man put his tongue between his teeth and sucked in air. His face became vicious.

'Manners, please. This is my abode – show some respect.' He turned to look at the boy, reached up and ran a hand through his hair. He turned back to Celeste. 'The boy is fine. I'm not the monster you think. I have no qualm with innocents.'

'Then just let him go.'

The man sucked in through his teeth again. 'It's not that simple.' He looked at Vangelis. 'Is it?'

Vangelis shuddered at the obsidian darkness in the man's eyes. 'Just tell us what you want. We'll do what we need to. Just let us take the boy and go.'

'That would be nice.' The man sneered. 'But I think you fail to appreciate the situation you are in.'

Vangelis tensed. 'I know what this is. We're in a computer program created by Vathos Systems. This is nothing more than a recreation of Hell. It's a damned program. All you have to do is open a back door and let us out.'

The man raised a thin black eyebrow. 'Is that all this is?' Slowly, he lifted his hand and extended a finger, on it a thick gold ring. He pointed the finger at Vangelis's chest. Vangelis felt a tight burning sensation in the middle of his chest, just above the sternum. It became tighter and tighter until he felt his skin crackle and tear. He tore open his shirt: a charred black wound had opened on his skin. Beneath it, blood bubbled. The man, still pointing, slowly lowered his finger; a black scar split open and traced its way down Vangelis's chest onto his belly. Vangelis screamed; Celeste reached out a hand, inadvertently putting a finger into the gaping wound. She recoiled and shrieked. The skin of Vangelis's chest fizzled and cracked, the wound opening deeper until his internal organs could be seen. The man in the silver suit, his face contorted in a kind of sick pleasure, closed his hand and pulled it away. Vangelis's head flicked back and his body spasmed, and when he looked down again the wound had closed. Vangelis ran a hand over his body, his breath heaving and his stomach muscles contracting with the strain. He pulled his shirt closed around him.

'Just a computer program…' The man put the cigarette between his lips, inhaled and blew out. 'How about I stub out this cigarette in your friend's empty eye-hole, see if it feels real?'

Vangelis, his breath still coming heavy, reached over and put a hand on Celeste's knee, as much for comfort as reassurance. He didn't say anything.

The man in the silver suit raised the cigarette to his mouth, but instead of puffing on it he turned it upside down and extinguished it on his tongue. Then he slipped it into his side pocket.

'What do you know of God?'

Neither Vangelis nor Celeste answered.

The man in the silver suit looked at Celeste. 'I suppose you lost any faith you had.' He grinned, then turned to Vangelis. 'You never had any to begin with. See, faith is like alcohol, or cigarettes. If you never had it, you never miss it. But once you start, it's hard to stop. They function the same way – they fill a hole, a void in the human soul. Man is born empty and spends his whole life looking for fulfillment.' He turned to Saleh and stroked his cheek. 'At least the smart ones do. The others, they spend their time denying fulfillment. Eh? Isn't that a tragedy. A whole life wasted trying to be good, or just, or chaste, when you could simply be out there indulging, trying anything to fill the emptiness that lies at the core of all of you.' The man sat back, bit his lower lip and looked at the ceiling. He sighed, as if burdened by an eons-old weariness. 'Of course, by saying all this I by no means deny there is a god.' He smirked. 'I know the cunt personally.' He let out a loud, violent groan. 'Christ, this is so tiresome. You people, you make me sick to my stomach.'

He stood up from the seat and turned around. Raising his hands to the ceiling he stretched, and yawned loudly and odiously. His jacket and shirt climbed his body to expose his lower back; Vangelis saw a network of black veins weave an ominous design over his skin. Then he let his arms fall, the strange markings covered once again. Without a pause, his back still to them, he opened his fly, took out his penis and began to piss.

'Yes, this God cunt… he's been on my back forever. But do you know what…' He looked over his shoulder to catch Vangelis's eye. '…There's not a goddamn thing he can do to me.' He winked. 'I'm untouchable. An outlier – master of my own kingdom.' He shook off and zipped up his fly. He turned around. 'I answer to no one.'

He stepped up behind Saleh, putting his hands on his shoulders, digging in his fingers. The boy gave a wince of pain. Celeste heard and tensed up. Then the man leaned down, putting his face into the boy's hair. He closed his eyes and inhaled. He whispered, 'Some things you never get tired of.'

Vangelis's hands tightened on the edge of his chair. The

man in the silver suit looked at him from the side of his eye.

'Wanna pick a fight with the Devil, son?' He turned back to the boy, put a hand on his cheek and stroked his face. 'You want the boy, you can have him.' He pulled out his chair and sat down again. 'All we need to do is negotiate.'

He closed his hands together and rested them on the table. Celeste spoke up.

'What is it you want?'

The man shrugged. 'Up to you – you need to come up with a price that satisfies me.'

Celeste turned her head to Vangelis. Then she turned back to the man in the silver suit.

'You can have me. Let the boy leave with him.'

The man grinned at Vangelis. 'Aren't mothers wonderful.' He turned back to Celeste. 'Do you know what you're proposing?'

'Yes.'

'No.' Vangelis put his hands on the table. 'You don't get her. You take me instead. The boy and the woman leave.'

The man sat back down and tucked two hands into his pants. He grinned, putting his tongue between his teeth and sucking in.

'Well aren't you two a couple of angels.'

He raised a hand into the air and clicked his fingers. Behind him a figure materialized, first vague and immaterial, then cohering until a dark, twisted-like being stood over the man in the silver suit. The figure had a body of charred and ruptured skin, eyes red, hands with stubs for fingers; in all other ways it resembled what might have once been a man.

Without looking behind him, the man indicated the being. 'This... this is what an angel looks like.'

The man then pointed to Celeste. The being came out from behind the chair and moved to the other side of the table. It hovered over Celeste for a moment. Vangelis made a move to protect her but the man raised a hand and caused a burning to shoot up Vangelis's esophagus. He doubled over in excruciating pain. Then the being reached down and took Celeste's face in its hands. A searing tore at her skin and she let out a cry. The being slid two charred fingers down her throat, causing her to gag. Then it lifted its other hand to its mouth. It retched several times, the muscles of its stomach tightening, then regurgitated a soft, white egg-like thing. Vangelis looked up to see the being take it between his fingers and force it into Celeste's gaping eye socket. It was an eye. Celeste screamed, the scream catching in her throat and turning into a bubbling, gargling sound, the being's fingers still in her throat. The dark angel forced the nerves and bloody sinew of her eye into the dark empty socket, until only white filled the hole in her skull. When he was done with one, he repeated the process with the other. Celeste's body bucked with the pain as she tried to escape the being's grip. When the second eye was entrenched in its socket, the dark angel extracted its black fingers from her throat. Celeste slipped to the floor.

The man in the silver suit released Vangelis from his death grip. Vangelis coughed and fell to his knees, before clambering up and putting an arm around Celeste. When she looked up into his face, she did so with two functioning bloodshot eyes.

'You okay?'

Celeste nodded, her face streaming with water that ran from her eyes. She put a hand on Vangelis's arm and pulled herself to her feet. She didn't sit down; instead, she stepped behind her chair defensively.

'I want out of here,' she croaked.

The man in the silver suit, now flanked by his dark angel, nodded. 'And you will. You will leave with the boy. But first you will watch his absolution.' He raised a finger and pointed at Vangelis. Vangelis put his hands on the table to stand up. The man turned his palm up and Vangelis's body went stiff, his back arched and the muscles in his neck taut. He let out a strained groan. Then the man raised his hand and Vangelis lifted off the floor several inches, his limbs splayed like some ghastly puppet.

'You chose this. Don't forget it.'

Celeste stepped back in horror. The man moved his hand, guiding Vangelis through the air until, with a violent snap of his hand, he thrust Vangelis down face-front onto the table.

'Why are you doing this!' Celeste shouted.

The man put a hand on Vangelis's shoulder and squeezed. The fabric of Vangelis's shirt began to smolder and he cried out in pain.

The man looked at her with dark finality. 'This is for you. So that you can leave. As you have requested.' He nodded. 'So it shall be.'

The man took Vangelis's shirt in two hands and ripped it from neck to hem, tearing it open to expose Vangelis's back. Vangelis tried to raise himself from the table but the man pinned his neck. He ran his other hand over the tattoo that covered Vangelis's back.

'Pretty picture.' He glanced at Celeste. 'Shame we're going to have to rip it off.'

Celeste began to back away but bumped into the dark angel who appeared behind her. Saleh stood unmoving, still in the thrall of their tormentor.

The man reached inside his jacket and took out a seax blade about eight inches long and with a handle of finely polished burl. Without ceremony, he pricked the skin of Vangelis's back just below the neck and ran it right down his spine. Vangelis screamed.

Celeste struggled to free herself from the dark angel. 'No, oh God no…'

The man then made a T-cut across Vangelis's shoulders. Vangelis gritted his teeth, hissed in pain. He fought, but the man's grip on his neck was fierce.

The man looked up at Celeste as he took a corner of the T-cut at the top of Vangelis's spine, and positioned the knife, poised to slice.

Celeste shook her head violently. 'No… you can't… I can't see this…'

She fought to turn her head, but the dark angel gripped her temples in his hands, his fingers pulling back the lids of her eyes. Wide-eyed in horror, she watched as the man dug his seax under the flesh and began to skin Vangelis's back.

The man worked roughly but studiously. 'This is real work. This is what it takes to make a man see. This is what needs to be done to bring a man around to the truth about himself. There is no other way.'

Vangelis's head bobbed off the table. His eyes bulged, the veins of his neck pulsed, he frothed at the mouth. All the while emitting a terrible hiss of pain. When the man had skinned back sufficient flesh that he could grip it with both hands, he took hold of it, and with a single yank, pulled. Flesh tore, a sound like ripping canvas. Vangelis let loose an unholy scream. The bared red flesh of his insides was exposed. Blood bubbled and squirted. The pale exposed muscles of his back pulsed and spasmed.

Then he did the other side. Vangelis passed out, but the man put a finger to his temple and immediately resuscitated him.

The two folds of his back were pulled open like two wings.

Celeste stook shaking uncontrollably in the hands of the dark angel, the face turned to the spectacle, the horror of it inescapable. The man in the silver suit looked at her and nodded solemnly.

The man was pleased with his work. He dropped the bloody seax onto the table and turned to Saleh. He took hold of the boy's face with his blood-soaked hand and directed it at the shuddering body on the table.

'See, boy? See what becomes of a man with no moral qualms? I get my way. I will always get my way.'

He ran a bloody hand down the boy's face, almost with affection.

Then he raised his head to the ceiling. Hooks appeared there, suspended on two wires. They lowered down to the level of the table.

Celeste, shriveled up inside herself, shuddered from her core.

The man took hold of one of the hooks. 'We will make of you a living tattoo,' he said. Thus spoken, he threaded the hook through one of the wings of Vangelis's back. Vangelis, barely conscious, merely trembled. The man threaded a hook through the other wing.

He looked at Celeste, opening his arms wide.

'And just like that, he was raised up…'

Pulled by unseen hands, the hooks rose. The wings of skin cut from Vangelis's back grew taut, then stretched. His body rose up off the table.

Celeste could only shake, her eyes still forced open to the sickening sight.

'No, no… God no…'

Vangelis was hoisted up until his two feet hung swinging above the table, the two folds of skin stretched out about him like the wings of some terrible angel. Blood ran down his legs and dripped onto the pristine white table.

The man in the silver suit closed his eyes and brought his two hands together reverentially.

'And like that, he was made holy…'

He opened his eyes to gaze upon the magnificence of his work. Then he turned to the boy. He placed a hand on his head.

'This man has sacrificed himself for you. Be released.'

Saleh was awoken from the thrall in which he languished. When his senses returned, he looked up to see the ripped and tortured body of Vangelis hanging over him. It took a moment for him to register what it was, but when he did, he stumbled back, knocking over the chair and falling to the ground with a cry.

The dark angel released Celeste. She fell to the floor, and scrambled on her hands and knees toward the boy. When she reached him, she threw her arms around him to protect him from the sight.

The man in the silver suit looked down at the two of them. The darkness of his being, the black abyss of his soul, drew the eyes of the woman and child on the floor. They looked up at him with terror and wonder.

The man, hands red, his silver suit smeared in the dark blood of his victim, nodded.

'Never forget what you have seen here today. Go in peace.'

8

The door to the oval room closed behind them. When Celeste turned around there was no longer a door to be seen. The man in the silver suit was gone. If she never saw him again, still he'd stain her memories until the day she died.

Celeste and Saleh stood in silence for a moment, stunned and scarred by what they'd witnessed. Slowly, their senses came back to them.

They were in a vast room like the main hall of a train station, but without windows. The walls and floor were obsidian black, and the hall was lined with seats carved of the same black stone. The seats were filled with dead souls like those Celeste had encountered by the lake of fire. These souls sat silently, a horrid vacuum emanating from their collective emptiness. The sight of them, so still and empty and void, filled Celeste with horror.

Saleh tugged on her arm. She looked down. He was holding out a tissue.

'Your eyes are leaking.'

Celeste put a hand to her face and found it damp. It wasn't tears… it was something else, a kind of mucus.

She took the tissue and dabbed her eyes.

Ahead of them, down the long room, the hall fell away into empty blackness. If there was a way out, it was that way.

Celeste took Saleh's hand. 'Come on. Let's get out of here.' They began to walk.

They made their way into the darkness, a sad and lonely march into further unknown, both carrying the terror that, after all this, they wouldn't be allowed to leave this godforsaken place. The weight of souls pressed in around them as they proceeded.

Then, without warning but as one, the dead souls rose to their feet, faces raised to the disorientated pair in the center of the hall. Celeste and Saleh looked around at the thousand faces – the blank hollow face of the lost, that disfeatured disk that spoke only of emptiness – turned upon them.

For a moment, neither of them moved.

Saleh whispered. 'What do they want?'

Celeste didn't reply.

Celeste raised her foot to take a step and the vast gathering made a move as one toward them.

'Maybe they're going to stop us from leaving.' Saleh's hand tightened around Celeste's. The vast multitude of the damned moved in concert, the circle tightening. As they neared, reaching about ten feet from the pair, as one they stopped. A long, imposing corridor of these lost souls reached away into the unknown. Then a soft murmur rose from them, a sound like the undulating of a sea of sorrow.

'They're not going to stop us,' Celeste said. 'They're lamenting that we're allowed to leave.'

She squeezed Saleh's hand and stepped forward. Saleh followed.

The multitude made no move closer, but their heads turned to follow the two exiles as they exited the place from which few ever returned. When they saw that they would not be impeded, Celeste and Saleh moved quicker. Unseeing faces followed them the whole way.

As they went, the darkness deepened, until they no longer saw the dead souls arrayed around them. But their song continued. Then, by degrees, the darkness inverted, and instead of walking into darkness deeper they found themselves walking toward a dim light. In the distance, then, they saw the door of an elevator.

Celeste shared a glance with Saleh, her heart quickening. Her palm was hot and sweaty against the boy's.

Their pace hastened them toward the elevator, the fear of an unknown something at their backs pursuing them all the way to the doors.

Celeste's fearful eyes met the boys as her hand reached for the single flashing button. Her finger hovered over it for a second, then with silent assent, she pushed.

The elevator dinged.

The doors opened. Inside, nothing lurked.

They stepped in.

They turned to look out into the vast darkness they'd just fled. The sorrowful lament of souls came at them in insistent waves as the doors closed.

Then they heard only the hum of the elevator as it began to rise.

Up it went. And up. For a long time. Each second like an eternity. Every second, escape seemed further away.

Then the elevator stopped.

The doors opened.

Sitting at a desk in a small, smoke-filled hallway was the yellow-suited man. He grinned, one leg draped lazily over the other, an elbow on his knee and in his raised, limp hand, a half-smoked cigarette.

'You got a hall pass,' he said, his voice cracked and phlegmy.

'Just let us out of here,' Celeste said, her voice somewhere between threatening and pleading.

'Uh-huh.' The man spoke slow and cockily. He raised two tobacco-stained fingers to his lips and took a puff, ash falling into his lap. He eyed the two fugitives. He grinned again, revealing dirty teeth. 'Quite the ride you've had, huh? I've seen people leave here before – not many, but some – and hell, they sure look ragged. But you two look real beat. I mean, you've been to the pits. You've been to the cellars, and now you get to breathe free air again. You know what I want to know…' He paused to suck on the cigarette, then pointed a brown finger at Celeste. '…I want to know what that first breath of free air tastes like, you know? That first suck of up-above air after you've been in the dungeons. And the light… what's that light gonna look like after you've swum the bitter darkness? Ya get me?'

He paused, thoughtful for a second, then he waved his hand, dropping more ash over the table.

'But who cares. This is my place. I know my home. And do you know what? I like it just fine.' He winked.

Celeste's hands trembled. 'Would you just open that door and let us out of here. Please.'

The man sneered, regarded her for a moment. Then he turned his attention to the desk, where a clipboard sat. He turned it around with stained fingers and thumb and jabbed at the page.

'Need your signature right here, ma'am,' he said. He extracted a pen from the inside pocket of his jacket, clicked it and laid it down.

Celeste looked at him for a moment, her eyes searching for any trace of duplicity or treachery. Then she picked up the pen and signed it in a trembling hand. She put down the pen.

The man turned the clipboard around. 'Aw, would you look at that. Isn't that cute. Like a child's hand.' He smirked, displaying a gross mouthful of teeth. He sat watching her for a moment as she struggled to control her shaking. Then he turned his eye on Saleh. 'Quite the woman, your mom.' He winked.

He turned and spat on the floor, and reached under the desk. Celeste heard the click of a button. The lock on the door disengaged.

She took Saleh's arm and pulled him toward it.

'Just one more thing…'

Celeste froze, turning her head in the direction of the man.

He waited until she made eye contact.

He raised his hand – cigarette now close to burning his fingers – to his head. He tapped his temple with a finger. 'We're always in here. We never leave. Don't be strangers.'

He smirked and waved to Saleh. 'See ya.'

Celeste turned and pulled Saleh through the door. As it closed behind them, Celeste fell to her hunkers and wrapped her arms around her shins, and wept profusely.

Saleh went down on one knee and put an arm around her shoulder. He said nothing, merely closed his eyes, feeling the heaving of her body against his.

Celeste reached up to take the hand that rested upon her shoulder. One by one she touched his thin fingers, feeling the coldness of his skin. It was reassuring nonetheless.

She raised her face to his, her face wet, her eyes bloodshot.

'Tell me you got what you went in there for?'

Saleh nodded. 'I got it.'

She squeezed his hand. 'Good.' Nodded. 'Good.'

She stood up and looked around. They were back in the garden of the estate where they'd entered the diabolical program. There was something unreal about her surroundings, an unreality she had not noticed before.

Then they both heard a voice in their heads.

—Jesus Christ… I found you. I got you both.

Celeste and Saleh heard the relief in those words. It was Eric.

—You okay?

'We're alive,' Celeste responded.

—Vangelis?

Neither answered. There was a pregnant silence from the other side.

—We're pulling you out. Right now.

Celeste turned to look at Saleh and caught his eye for a split second before there was a blinding flash and a searing rush at the base of her skull.

She opened her eyes to a painful sensation of light.

Celeste sat watching as the needle was inserted into Saleh's arm. The boy lay on a cot in a Vathos safehouse. It was sparse, devoid of any permanent presence, much like any other base she'd seen that the small marauding resistance kept. If they needed to they could get out fast, destroying with minimum difficulty any trace they'd ever been there.

Eve was drawing blood from the boy, while Verne sat by with a compact hematology analysis kit hooked up to his laptop.

'What are they doing?' Celeste said softly. 'Do I need to do it too?'

Eric glanced at her and back to the boy.

'While he was inside he located the information we asked of him – or at least he thinks he did. He said he was given a SIM card while he was down there, and that he swallowed it. We're not sure, but the only thing we can think happened is the information he discovered was imprinted, or somehow encoded, into his DNA. We have the Vathos digital signatures from the program you recovered for us, so once we have the blood sample we just need to run a search. Should show up the signatures pretty quickly.' He paused. 'If they're there.'

Eric folded his arms, eyes still on Saleh. The boy's face was drawn and tired, and his eyes had a far-away look that Celeste could fathom, but Verne could only guess at.

'I can't imagine what the two of you experienced down there.' He turned to her, to see if he might elicit a response. None came. 'It must have been… hell.'

Celeste shook her head, then glanced at him before turning her face away. 'I might tell you about it. Someday. But not for a long time.'

Eric nodded. He turned back to the operation before him. From where they leaned against the counter, they could see the laptop terminal run the results of Saleh's blood analysis through the DNA sequencer. They were only waiting a minute or two before the search came back with a result.

Verne looked over his shoulder to catch Eric's eye. He nodded. Verne took a few steps forward to come up behind him. Celeste moved next to them.

Eric folded his arms, his head craning to get a look at the screen. 'What is it? What've you got?'

Verne pointed a lazy finger in the direction of the laptop screen. 'There it is.' He shook his head. 'Fucking incredible. Written right into his DNA.'

Eric clenched a fist. He glanced at Celeste then back at the screen.

'It's all there? Everything we need?'

'We haven't opened the content yet, but it's Vathos. Signature's all over it.' He turned to look at Eric emphatically. 'Right off their servers.'

'Motherfuckers,' Verne whispered. 'I think we got em.'

9

A silence pregnant with the excitement of violence permeated a small room of the security wing where two men watched a screen intently.

Rodin, head of security, sat in a chair in front of two displays. Behind him, arms folded and with two fingers pulling on his lip nervously, Emerson. One screen, the display for live running programs, now showed only static. The other showed a figure, unmoving, seemingly unconscious, in an insertion chair. That figure was Vangelis Zervas.

'Vitals?' Emerson's voice was tinged with anxiety.

Rodin didn't look up. 'There's a pulse. Just. Another two minutes in there and he might be dead.'

'Son of a bitch survived.' Emerson shook his head and looked away for a second, as if contemplating the repercussions of this development. He scratched the back of his neck.

Rodin looked over his shoulder at Emerson. 'We can't leave him alive.'

Emerson shook his head. 'No.' He paused. 'But we could hang onto him for another month or two, keep him sedated and run him through a few more test programs. May as well get something back for our investment.'

Rodin nodded. 'Maynes would just love that.'

Emerson tugged at an ear. 'Yeah, well. This place wouldn't

run without the sickos.'

A face appeared on the screen in front of Rodin. It was Maynes.

'Sir, subject is out. He's in bad shape, but he's still breathing. What do I do with him?'

Rodin glanced at Emerson, then pushed a button on the console. 'Take him to recovery. Get medical have a look at him.'

Maynes raised an eyebrow, at which Emerson leaned over Rodin's shoulder to speak. 'Do as Rodin says. We keep him alive.'

'Sir.' Maynes turned around.

Rodin punched a button and the screen went blank. He turned around on his swivel chair then stood up. 'I'll go get started on the diagnostics report. Give us forty-eight hours for a full rundown?'

Emerson nodded. 'Send the telemetry straight to Analytics. Just get me the core operational data.'

'I'll draft in a few extra hands to assist with the processing. There's a lot of new information here.'

'Right then…' Emerson turned and opened the door. '…I'll give it an hour or two then go pay a visit to our lab rat.'

A corner of Rodin's mouth twitched. 'If he's still alive.'

Maynes stood in the bathroom of the Subversion floor, hands on the sink, eyes locked onto his reflection in the mirror, a thousand-yard stare in his eyes. He was elsewhere. In another place, another time. His face was flecked with red and his thick boxer's nose flared. A thick vein in his right temple filled with blood and stood out from his head, then settled, only to throb again seconds later. His eyes had a redness to them, not borne of tiredness but some indefinable torment deep inside. His jaw tensed and the muscles of his neck flared, then his tongue darted out to flick over his lower lip, hanging there grotesquely for a long moment. He coughed, a sharp hacking cough ripped from somewhere down in his diaphragm. His face swelled up and his eyes bulged from his head. Spittle shot from his mouth and speckled the mirror; he wiped his mouth with his forearm before breaking into a new bout of coughing.

A pause. He turned on the tap and splashed water into his mouth and over his face and spat in the sink. Drool hung from his lips. He looked up from the sink into the mirror once more; a lizard blackness seemed to flash over his eyes. Then he doubled over, hissing in agony at some unnamed affliction. Straightening up, he ripped off his jacket and pulled aside his tie, before tearing his shirt open to expose a corpulent belly. He scratched at it, staring at it in the mirror before lowering his eyes to look at it direct. Suddenly paranoid, he looked over his shoulder; he was alone, certainly there wasn't anyone in the cubicles behind him. The only noise was the sound of the air conditioning running above his head. A long, pained grunt issued from him; his face was swollen now with the dark thing being birthed within him. Two thick hands scratched his belly raw, before the affliction crawled upward. He clutched his chest now, scratching, raising bloody welts on his skin. His face throbbed, spittle flecked his chin and lips, his eyes flashed reptile-like as he stared wide-eyed and terrified in the mirror at his contortions. Choking now, he put two hands around his throat as if that might somehow relieve the constriction. He gagged. Then again. Something, some dark humor from deep down leaked from his mouth. It dropped into the sink, a strange mixture of black, red, yellow and green, and lay there, gross omen that something was not right with him.

Then it came. First a tail-like appendage which dangled from his mouth and seemed to move, flicker, as if imbued with a life of its own. He gawped at it in the mirror, terror in his eyes. More of it slid from his mouth, black and slick, like a huge worm that pulsed hideously. Its girth about three inches in diameter at its middle, it stole from his mouth until all foot and a half of it plopped into the sink like a freak stillborn. But this thing was not dead. It squirmed, testing the confines of its cradle, then, finding the hole, poked one end of its body into the plughole. Maynes watched in horror. The huge black worm worked its fat body into the hole entire, then with a final flick of the tail, was gone.

Maynes spun around once more, eyes to the door. He turned on the water and washed the bile away, ripping a sheaf of paper from the dispenser and wiping the sink frantically. He tossed the paper in the bin. Looking up at his reflection in the mirror now, he saw how disheveled and wild his appearance. He gave his face a splash of water and dried it, and dabbed his reddened and streaked torso. As best he could he closed up his shirt and righted his tie, then picked up his jacket and slipped it on. He buttoned it up. With a final look in the mirror he ran a hand through his thinning hair, pausing a moment to stare at his reddened eyes. Then he turned and went out.

'Where the hell you been?'

No sooner in the hallway than accosted.

'I been looking all over for you.'

'Sir.' Maynes nodded, lowering his eyes for a second. 'Nature calling.'

Emerson took a long look at him, eyes roving from his face to his crumpled appearance. 'You alright?'

'Yes sir. Came over a bit peaky is all. That was a tough run.'

'Yeah?' Emerson raised an eyebrow. 'Clearly you need a spell in recovery too.'

Maynes coughed, and nodded. 'Yes sir. I will. Soon as I finish up here.'

Emerson looked over Maynes's shoulder down the hall. 'You have him inside?'

'Yes sir.'

'Take me to see him.'

Maynes nodded and turned on his heels, and led Emerson down the hall. At the end he stopped at a door, glanced at his boss, then opened it. Emerson followed him in and Maynes closed the door.

A medical attendant turned to look over her shoulder as they entered, before turning back to her patient, parting his eyelids with thumb and forefinger and shining a light in his eye. She scribbled something on a clipboard then turned, putting the clipboard on a counter. With a small flick of the head Maynes instructed her to give them a moment. She nodded, going into a side room.

In the middle of the room strapped to a standing gurney was Vangelis Zervas. He was unconscious, stripped to all but his underwear. Emerson turned to look at Maynes.

'This is your idea of recovery?'

Maynes cleared his throat. 'Sir, we wanted to be sure we'd extracted everything before dispensing with him. Extraordinary methods may be required.'

'You mean 'torture'.'

'*Extraction*, sir.'

'Uh-huh.' Emerson took a good look at Zervas. He took a deep breath and sighed. 'Well, whatever you need to do. This is expired merchandise now.'

'Yes sir.'

Emerson flicked a wrist and looked at his watch. 'I've given Analytics forty-eight hours for their report, but I'll expect yours by tomorrow. Make sure it's on my desk by close.'

'I'll have it ready, sir.'

'Good. I'm going home.' He looked from Emerson to Zervas once more, before turning and going out the door.

Maynes turned and looked at his underling. The attendant came out of the room, stopping behind Maynes. Maynes turned his head.

'That's fine, you can go now. I got it from here.'

'Yes sir.' The attendant picked up the clipboard, signed it and put it down. Then she went out. The door closed softly behind her.

He stood and looked at Vangelis Zervas for a long time. A heart monitor hooked up to the patient beeped intermittently, and soon the beep seemed to beat with an intensity that made his brain throb. Maynes took a few steps toward Zervas until he was so close he was almost touching. His tongue came out of his mouth again in the same gross manner, and he gagged, as if getting ready to expel another fat black worm. Then he recovered.

He leaned forward until his mouth was at Zervas's ear. 'You in there fucker?' When there was no response, Maynes pressed his face into Zervas's, until his nose was squashed up against his captive's ear like a pig's. 'I said are in you in there fucker?'

Zervas didn't move. Maynes pulled away and took Zervas's face in his hand, and squeezed his cheeks until his tongue pushed from his mouth. Maynes stuck out his own tongue in imitation.

Then he snorted, leaned in and licked Zervas's face with his fat tongue. When he spoke, it was with a Southern accent that was not his own.

'You done think you met the Devil… son, we gon' dance some more. We ain't done, you and me. We's tied, you and me.'

His eyes flashed a reptile blackness.

CONTINUE WITH PART FIVE...

THE SISTEMA SERIES

1. CEREBRUM

Subconscious torture for political and corporate subversion. That's the trade of Vathos—creeping into a target's dreams to force the shady ends of their clients. It's dirty business.

Vangelis Zervas is one of their Subversion agents and makes a living inflicting pain on people in their sleep. A recipient of the most stringent training and a man of few qualms, he'll do whatever it takes to get the job done. But when a series of events calls his dedication into question, strange things begin to happen when he infiltrates the dreams of his targets. Soon he's asking himself—is it he in the mark's head, or is someone else in his?

A no-holds-barred dystopian horror that will put your teeth on edge.

2. ACOLYTE

Caleb, a young school dropout, robs an apartment one night with his petty-criminal friend, Vince. Finding an expensive and rare piece of computer hardware, he pockets it, oblivious to its power and purpose. The boy plugs himself into the new device, unaware that the program inside it is a diabolical piece of software, one which almost kills him. But those who created the program do not want it out in the world and will do anything to retrieve it, including killing anyone in whose possession it is found. Caleb may find that by taking the device he has unwittingly unleashed forces that will consume all he knows and loves.

3. CHIMERA

Following the murder of her young son, Celeste goes all in with a group of co-conspirators to infiltrate Vathos, the company she believes responsible for the death of her child. The faction make tentative contact with Vangelis Zervas, hoping he will help them penetrate the Vathos servers so they may gather evidence to bring the company down. Despite the nature of his ruthless and horrific work, Vangelis may have his own misgivings with the company. But is it enough for him to turn on Vathos?

In the end, he may have only one choice: Hell or death.

4. Inferno

After a penetration operation on the Vathos servers goes awry, Celeste and Vangelis Zervas are cast into the Vathos mainframe following a possible sabotage operation from within the company. The pair are drawn into the 'Inferno' program, a devious piece of software long held in the companies archives, the program a digitalized recreation of Hell itself. Celeste and Zervas are pursued by Maynes, who, having discovered that the agent has gone rogue, is hell-bent on retribution. But no one gets through Inferno unscathed. Evil begets evil, and soon Celeste and Zervas will come face to face with something far darker, and far more sinister than Maynes.

5. Diablo

Within every man is a devil. There is only one Satan.

Vangelis Zervas has just been subjected to the most insidious psychological program ever invented by man. He comes out of it in a coma, sequestered in the Medical wing at Vathos systems. Maddox Maynes, his supervising officer, has also returned from their encounter in 'Inferno', still conscious but carrying something deeply sinister within him. The reverberations of the program are carried from the virtual into the real, as Vathos is shaken from within by the greatest enemy it will ever face. This is the beginning of the end.

LITTLE SWINE

A small basement cell. A dirty bed. A chair.

These are the confines of Little Swine's world. Prisoner of Momma and subject to the tortures of Boy, her life is a living hell.

Momma has a plan. Momma wants a baby that she may redeem the sins of her past. This is Little Swine's purpose. And when Momma has what she wants, Little Swine will be discarded.

But violence begets violence and blood begets blood, and many will die before the devil has his quota. One can never underestimate the power of retribution.

THE COTTAGE

Men are men until they encounter evil. And after, they are compelled to do evil itself.

Turning their backs on New York, John and Katie Mears purchase their dream home in colonial Connecticut, the place they hope to raise their firstborn and build life as a family. But the cradle of the American nation has a haunting past, and they find themselves swallowed by a dark history, one of blood and anguish, a specter of the country's painful birth in the slaughter of pilgrim times. The dark crucible of the nation is yet manifest. Blood debt is eternal, and sooner or later history calls for retribution. It is the blood of innocents that pays for the sins of the father.

MEAT

In the murky wake of the financial crisis a string of establishments pop up across Europe catering to a hedonistic underground, its clientele beholden to a strange, hallucinatory meat. Stoked by the fleshy and charismatic Hugo and fuelled by voracious consumption of ecstasy, the craze spreads from the heart of Europe all the way to the Mediterranean, where in Athens the financial elite begin to turn on each other. Murder, barbecue and apocalyptic raving ensues, culminating in the most savage party Mykonos has ever seen. Follow the story to its destructive end, where consumption eats itself alive.

NOTES FROM A CANNIBALIST

1847. Assuming the identity of a dead Jesuit priest, a survivor of the famine in Ireland travels to South America where he is tasked with rebuilding the missions among the natives. Inducted into local life, Father James Carmichael finds love with a native woman and becomes acquainted with the ways of the Guaraní, discovering ayahuasca and ritualism. In a battle with his own gods and demons, the priest fights for the life he envisions, his own self the ultimate stake of the struggle. Worlds are shattered, realities crumbled, lives destroyed. His soul victim to the crucible of the New World, what is tempered in the chaos will be outside his control.

A WHORE'S SONG

Hidden away in the backstreets of Amsterdam is a secretive whorehouse, open only to those in the know, where torture, pain and extreme sexual sport are the vehicle to understanding and self-knowledge. Run by the obscure Madame Zhu, the establishment is a magnet to the city's elite and mad soul-seekers alike. Two lives collide in a chaotic downward spiral brought about by psychoactives and sexual torture when, over the course of a day, a whore recounts her life as a destroyer of egos and one man is forced to face his deepest demons. Cast out into the far reaches of his mind, will he make it back from the other side?

In a world where the weak become prey and strength means brutality, living may come at the cost of dying first.

The Book of God

God isn't dead. He's just a bit mental...

Indignant at his corrupt and ignominious creation, God sits and stews in his treehouse outside the small town of Brawl. His only companion and sole remaining attendant, a withered and tortured scribe, chronicles the Lord's descent into madness as he struggles to collect all the lost souls which have escaped his records and further addled the Lord's already woolly mind. But when the Scribe is forced to hire a maid to care for the Almighty, the introduction of a buxom woman into God's life brings chaos in its wake. And what's more, the maid has an innocent and attractive young daughter...

Suffering rejection, humiliation and loathing of humankind, God seeks a way to bring back Christ and trigger the Apocalypse. The only thing standing in his way? God's old harpy of a mother...

The Jaguar

1849. Salome Azul, daughter of a powerful politician, flees Buenos Aires at the height of the Argentinian civil war. In London she enlists the help of Irishman Sean Ryan to open The Nightingale, a high-class brothel and opium den that will be used to entrap and blackmail London's political elite.

In doing so she will make enemies. What's more, Ms. Azul has carried her own demons from Argentina, and it is these that will prove her most relentless foe. In order to survive, she must eliminate all weakness from her character. Doing so may mean cutting away all she cherishes most.

In the pursuit of power, unrelenting sacrifice is what decides who lives and dies.

WORKS OF TRANSLATION BY ULTAN BANAN

Pietro Aretino's Dialogues

Nanna has been a nun. She's been a wife. She has also been a courtesan. And now, as her daughter turns sixteen, she must decide how to advise on her path in life. On what route should she send young Pippa?

Bawdy, filthy, hilarious and uproarious, listen to Nanna regale her friend Antonia with scandalous tales—tales of seduction, blasphemy, lies, dishonesty, thievery, nastiness, cruelty and treachery—in an attempt to decide on what course to set her daughter: should she be a nun, a wife or a whore?

Ultan Banan started writing as a way of getting his head straight, discovering in the process that staying busy is the only way to stop oneself going insane. He devotes what time he can to writing, doing his best to avoid gainful employment by increasingly creative means. He lives on the move but dreams of a small cottage on a foul and inhospitable coast somewhere. Currently in Scotland.

Latest news at
ultanbanan.com

Substack:
ultanbanan.substack.com

Twitter:
twitter.com/ultanbanan